SECRET MANTRAS FOR SUCCESS

PROSPECTUS OF PROFESSIONAL PEACE

SUDHANSHU SRIVASTAVA

Copyright © Sudhanshu Srivastava
All Rights Reserved.

This book has been self-published with all reasonable efforts taken to make the material error-free by the author. No part of this book shall be used, reproduced in any manner whatsoever without written permission from the author, except in the case of brief quotations embodied in critical articles and reviews.

The Author of this book is solely responsible and liable for its content including but not limited to the views, representations, descriptions, statements, information, opinions and references ["Content"]. The Content of this book shall not constitute or be construed or deemed to reflect the opinion or expression of the Publisher or Editor. Neither the Publisher nor Editor endorse or approve the Content of this book or guarantee the reliability, accuracy or completeness of the Content published herein and do not make any representations or warranties of any kind, express or implied, including but not limited to the implied warranties of merchantability, fitness for a particular purpose. The Publisher and Editor shall not be liable whatsoever for any errors, omissions, whether such errors or omissions result from negligence, accident, or any other cause or claims for loss or damages of any kind, including without limitation, indirect or consequential loss or damage arising out of use, inability to use, or about the reliability, accuracy or sufficiency of the information contained in this book.

Made with ♥ on the Notion Press Platform
www.notionpress.com

To my loving and caring wife,Namrata

Your unwavering support and inspiration have been the guiding light behind this book. Thank you for encouraging me to share the successful outcomes of my long experiences. This book is a testament to your belief in me and our journey together.

With all my love and gratitude

Contents

Foreword

In the fast-paced world of modern professional life, the pursuit of success often seems to come at the expense of inner peace. Many of us find ourselves constantly striving to climb the corporate ladder, meet deadlines, and achieve our career goals, only to feel increasingly disconnected and overwhelmed. It is in this context that "Secret Mantras for Success: Prospectus of Professional Peace" emerges as a beacon of hope and guidance.

Sudhanshu, an esteemed journalist and a scholar of human behavior, has dedicated over four decades to understanding the intricacies of professional success and personal fulfillment. Drawing from his vast reservoir of experience, he has distilled his insights into powerful, actionable sutras that offer a holistic approach to achieving both professional excellence and inner tranquility.

This book is not just a collection of career tips and strategies; it is a transformative guide that integrates timeless wisdom with contemporary practices. Each sutra is crafted to help you navigate the challenges of the workplace while fostering a sense of harmony and peace within yourself. What makes these sutras truly remarkable is their uniqueness—many of them offer perspectives and techniques that are rarely taught in conventional training programs or workshops.

"Secret Mantras for Success: Prospectus of Professional Peace" challenges the notion that success and peace are mutually exclusive. Through its pages, Sudhanshu invites you to embark on a journey of self-discovery and growth, where small changes in your mindset and behavior can create profound positive impacts in your professional and personal life.

As you go into this book, you will find that it is more than just a guide; it is a companion that empowers you to achieve your highest potential while maintaining a balanced and fulfilling life. Sudhanshu's belief that a little change within can create wonders around you is a powerful testament to the transformative potential within each of us.

I am confident that this book will inspire you and provide you with the tools and insights needed to navigate your professional journey with grace, resilience, and peace. It is an honor to present to you "Secret Mantras for Success: Prospectus of Professional Peace."

Sincerely,
Swami Muktanand
New Jersey

Preface

The professional world is a complex and dynamic expanse, one that I have navigated for over four decades. Throughout my career, I have had the unique opportunity to work at various levels within numerous organizations, from local firms to multinational corporations. This extensive journey has provided me with a deep understanding of the diverse challenges and opportunities that professionals encounter.

During my career, I have had the privilege of working with 24 different bosses and interacting with hundreds of colleagues, subordinates, and top executives. Each interaction has enriched my understanding of human behavior in the workplace and has contributed to the development of the principles that form the foundation of this book. These experiences, both as an employee and a leader, have allowed me to observe firsthand the qualities that lead to professional success and personal fulfillment.

"Secret Mantras for Success: Prospectus of Professional Peace" is the culmination of these experiences. The sutras within this book are not just theoretical concepts but are practical, well-tested principles that I have refined over years of practice. These sutras were born out of real-world interactions and challenges, and they have been proven to help individuals excel in their professional lives while maintaining a sense of inner peace.

In my early years, I was driven by ambition and the desire to climb the corporate ladder. As an employee, I observed the behaviors and strategies of my peers and superiors, learning from their successes and mistakes. These experiences taught me the importance of adaptability, resilience, and continuous learning.

As I progressed into leadership roles, I encountered a new set of challenges. Leading teams and managing people required a different skill set—one that involved empathy, effective communication, and ethical decision-making. My interactions with subordinates and colleagues of various personalities and backgrounds helped me develop a more nuanced understanding of what it takes to be a successful leader.

Throughout my career, I have seen the impact of stress, burnout, and conflict on professional performance and personal well-being. I realized that true success is not just about achieving career milestones but also about finding balance and peace in one's work-life ecosystem. This realization led me to explore and integrate practices that promote mental well-being and harmony, alongside traditional measures of success.

"Secret Mantras for Success: Prospectus of Professional Peace"offers a holistic approach to professional development. Each sutra is designed to address different aspects of professional life, from goal setting and productivity to leadership and ethical decision-making. What sets these sutras apart is their emphasis on achieving success without sacrificing personal well-being. They offer a roadmap to navigating the complexities of the professional world while maintaining a sense of inner tranquility.

I believe that while we may not always be able to change our external circumstances, we have the power to transform our internal landscapes. By making small, intentional changes within ourselves, we can create a ripple effect that positively impacts our surroundings. This book is my attempt to share the wisdom I have gained through my professional journey, with the hope that it will help you find both success and peace in your own career.

Thank you for embarking on this journey with me. May the Mantras in this book guide you towards a fulfilling and harmonious professional life.

Sincerely,

Sudhanshu

Acknowledgements

Writing "Secret Mantras for Success: Prospectus of Professional Peace" has been a deeply enriching experience, and I am immensely grateful to the many individuals who have supported and inspired me throughout this journey.

First and foremost, I want to express my heartfelt gratitude to my loving and caring wife. Your unwavering support, patience, and encouragement have been the cornerstone of this book. Your belief in my work and your continuous inspiration have driven me to share my experiences and insights with others.

I am also profoundly thankful to my 24 bosses and the countless colleagues, subordinates, and executives I have worked with over the past four decades. Each of you has contributed to my understanding of professional success and personal fulfillment. Your interactions, whether challenging or supportive, have shaped the sutras in this book and provided valuable lessons that I am honored to share.

To the organizations, both local and multinational, that I have had the privilege of being a part of—thank you for providing diverse and dynamic environments that fostered my growth and development. Each organization played a vital role in expanding my perspective and honing the principles presented in this book.

A special thanks to my mentors and peers in the fields of journalism and human behavior. especially Mr Shashi Sheekhr ,His insights and guidance have been invaluable, helping me to distill complex ideas into practical, actionable sutras that can benefit others.

I am also grateful to my readers, whose curiosity and desire for professional and personal growth have motivated me to put pen to paper. Your feedback and engagement are the ultimate reward for this endeavor.

Lastly, I would like to acknowledge the support of my publishing team. Your expertise, dedication, and belief in this project have been instrumental in bringing this book to life.

Thank you all for being a part of this journey. Your contributions have made "Secret Mantras for Success: Prospectus of Professional Peace" a reality, and I am deeply appreciative of your support.

Sincerely,

Sudhanshu

Prologue

In the dimly lit room, raindrops tapped on the windowpane like a melancholic melody, echoing the somber mood that enveloped my mind. The events of the previous night replayed in my thoughts, a heated exchange with my boss that left a bitter taste lingering in the air. The possibility of resignation loomed over me, a daunting choice between self-respect and survival.

Lost in my turmoil, I sat at my desk, penning down the grievances and injustices I had endured. The decision to walk away seemed inevitable, though the path ahead seemed treacherous. As I sifted through the storm of conflicting emotions, a knock at the door disrupted my thoughts.

"Sir, will you have some tea?" my peon inquired.

A reluctant "yes" escaped my lips. In moments, a steaming cup of double-dip typical Indian chai appeared on my desk, enveloping the room in a comforting aroma. I stared at the cup, transfixed by the swirling tendrils of steam, contemplating the warmth that beckoned from within.

In that moment of indecision, I took the first sip. The heat touched my lips, traveled down my throat, and settled warmly in my stomach. It wasn't just hot; it was a paradoxical blend of warmth and coolness, a harmonious melody that mirrored the complexities of my own emotions.

As I sipped, the essence of the tea seeped into my being. The turmoil within me began to subside, replaced by a newfound clarity. With each sip, the bitter thoughts and resentment transformed into an objective introspection.

The tea acted as a catalyst, unleashing a metamorphosis within.

I pondered over my grievances and questioned the righteousness of my actions. The waves of objectivity, fueled by the tea, reshaped my perspective. It became evident that I had overlooked the positive aspects of my relationship with my boss. He was the one who had recognized my potential, promoting me thrice in the past five years.

With the last sip, a sense of resolution enveloped me. The warmth of the tea had not only comforted my body but also thawed the icy barriers within my mind. I felt compelled to mend the fractured relationship with my boss.

Leaving my desk, I approached his room, the mug still cradled in my hands. As I entered, an apology hung in the air. The words spilled out, fueled by the transformative power of the tea. To my surprise, my boss rose from his chair, a softened expression on his face. He hugged me and admitted, "No dear, even I was not right. I am sorry too."

In that moment, i was still confused about what rfeally, worked as magic, turning the bitterness of conflict into a cup brimming with understanding and reconciliation. The rainy day had washed away the storm within, leaving behind a renewed sense of connection and a story that would soon find its way into the pages of this book.

As I embarked on my journey to explore and cultivate peace in the professional world, this experience became the catalyst for developing the sutras that you will discover within these pages. They are not just principles; they are tools, like that cup of tea, designed to cool tempers, foster productivity, and bring about lasting peace in our work-life ecosystem.

The realization dawned upon me that if something as simple and commonplace as tea could have such a profound impact on restoring harmony and clarity in a moment of conflict, then surely there must be other tools, rituals, and practices that could similarly transform the workplace. Thus began my quest to observe and understand every nuance of behavior in the office environment.

I started noticing the realms of anger that could erupt over minor issues, the conflicts driven by moods and misunderstandings, and the fragile egos that often obscured genuine intentions. I observed how these dynamics played out not only between colleagues but also within teams and across hierarchies in organizations of all sizes—from bustling startups to established multinational corporations.

What struck me most profoundly was the realization that many conflicts arose not from inherent malice but from a lack of effective communication, emotional intelligence, and a shared understanding of goals and values. Egos, I found, were often inflated by insecurity or fear rather than genuine authority or expertise.

Armed with this insight, I began to develop and refine the sutras—practical principles and strategies—that could mitigate these conflicts, promote collaboration, and cultivate a culture of mutual respect and productivity. These sutras were born from my interactions with hundreds of individuals whose behaviors and attitudes shaped my understanding of what it means to thrive in a professional environment.

In this book, "Secret Mantras for Success: Prospectus of Professional Peace" I share with you the culmination of my observations, experiences, and learnings. These sutras are not mere theories but practical tools crafted to empower you to navigate the complexities of professional life with grace and wisdom.

Join me on this journey as we uncover these secrets together and embark on a transformative path towards achieving professional peace and personal fulfillment.

Sudhanshu

CHAPTER ONE

Lessons of the Life

In my professional journey spanning four decades, every twist and turn, every triumph and setback, has been a stepping stone to wisdom. This Book is a culmination of those 40 years, each experience etching lessons that shimmer with insight. With a wealth of interactions with over 1500 professionals, I bring forth a treasure trove of time-tested hacks, invaluable tricks, and pragmatic practices that will undoubtedly shape your path to success.

I have already mentioned a lot more strategies, tricks, hacks, and practices in the previous chapters. In the following pages, you will find a few more very worth reading treasure trove of knowledge distilled from the realms of personal experience, research, and interactions with a vast array of professionals. These insights are more than mere theories – they're the embodiment of what works and what doesn't, garnered from the vast landscape of human interactions and corporate dynamics.

Relevance of these sutras

Why the Sutras I am going to describe in this chapter are important. These are not only important but vital and the only hope for employees and managers who are the victims of bad bosses. Before going to sutrass let us look into the following authentic research findings regarding the world's most developed economy, the guiding force behind the universal development. Any idea about how much the big companies in US are spending to cool down the heat created by these unruly bad bosses? Not less than $15 billion.

And the surprising fact is, even though companies invest a significant amount of money, around $15 billion every year, in training and developing managers and leaders to create a cool productive -congenial ecosystem, there is still a prevalent issue of having ineffective and negative bosses in the American workplace. Research conducted by Life Meets Work discovered that 56% of employees in the United States consider their boss to have a negative impact, ranging from somewhat harmful to highly detrimental.

Furthermore, a separate study conducted by the American Psychological Association revealed that a substantial 75% of Americans identify their supervisor as the primary source of stress during their workday. you cannot imagine the extent of bitterness created by bad bosses in countries like India.

To cool this heat, I have already given a lot of hacks and tricks in the chapters so far. In this chapter, You will get a few more Hacks for Thriving in the Corporate Jungle/ Unveiling productivity secrets/ Discover the subtle art of managing time, tasks, and energy to amplify your efficiency and impact.

Dealing with techniques that transform everyday interactions into power-packed tools for influence and understanding. Challenges are opportunities I will try to explain to you the Tricks for Transforming Challenges into Opportunities/ The adversity advantage/Learn how challenges can be turned into catalysts for personal growth and innovation. Few tips and strategies for problem-solving / Explore techniques for dissecting complex problems, identifying solutions, and steering towards success.

Practices for Nurturing Professional Growth will also be there / Embark on a journey of perpetual self-improvement through research, education, and embracing change. / Cultivating resilience and adaptability/Developing a toolkit to weather storms and evolve gracefully in the face of change will also be there. You will get the essence of the Insights from more than 1500 Professional Interactions/ Unveiling patterns of success /Peer into the experiences and trajectories of a diverse range of professionals to discern the common threads that weave success stories / Lessons from failures: Embrace the shared experiences of professionals who've triumphed over adversity, extracting wisdom from their setbacks. Craft your success These tricks and hacks will help you in

Crafting your success roadmap:

Distill the insights provided in this chapter into a personalized plan for achieving your career aspirations / implementing change/Learn how to apply these hacks, tricks, and practices in your professional journey to yield tangible, transformative results. As you traverse the pages that follow, envision each nugget of wisdom as a compass guiding you through the intricacies of the professional landscape.

These insights have been curated not just from the archives of my journey, but from the vast tapestry of experiences woven by professionals across diverse industries. With the culmination of 40 years of dedication, perseverance, and interaction with over 1500 professionals, I present to you a chapter that is not just about knowledge, but about empowerment. Let's embark on this journey of growth and transformation together, armed with the collective wisdom that will redefine your trajectory to success.

CHAPTER TWO

Cripple your Boss

HR people will call this sutra unethical but let them cry, Nothing wrong in it. I practiced this successfully.Top bosses are already using this technique to please their bosses. Do it and see the amazing results and enjoy the growth.

The phrase "cripple your boss with your hard work" may sound confrontational, but my request is to examine it in a constructive light, it emphasizes the impact of dedication and excellence in the workplace. Rather than taking a negative or adversarial approach, the essence of this idea lies in demonstrating your value, skills, and commitment to your role in a way that positively influences your boss and the overall dynamics of the organization.

Let me tell you the story of the invention of this Sutras. The "Cripple Your Boss" sutras took shape during my time at an electrifying electronic media company, where I found myself under the thumb of a formidable and demanding boss. Being a newcomer to the world of media, my background in print media unexpectedly became my beacon of wisdom. It was in this environment that I faced the relentless storm of my bullying boss, a tempest of insults and taunts that seemed ceaseless.

But within me, a decision crystallized like a lightning bolt – a fork in the road where I had to choose my path. I decided to take the reins, and I hatched the "Cripple Your Boss" strategy, haunting me since long, this strategy was not about causing harm, but rather about seizing control of my circumstances. With determination burning like a fire within, I began my quest. Armed with a notepad, I embarked on the journey of understanding my boss's quirks. I painstakingly recorded the top 15 aspects of my assigned tasks that seemed to irk my boss, like thorns in their side. Additionally, I scrutinized the top five elements that held paramount importance in the eyes of my boss's superiors – the key levers that commanded attention.

And then, like a craftsman molding clay, I refocused my efforts. I relinquished the haphazard juggling of tasks and instead directed my energies like a laser beam. I tackled the tasks that ticked off my boss from my list of 15 challenges. Furthermore, I set my sights on the five pivotal elements that captured the attention of my boss's higher-ups, thus aligning my actions with their aspirations. The transformation was nothing short of astounding. The "Cripple Your Boss" approach became my compass, leading me through the labyrinth of office politics and power dynamics. As I seized the reins of my own destiny, my boss's once intimidating presence began to wane, and a newfound equilibrium emerged.

In the end, this wasn't a tale of harm but a tale of empowerment – where seizing control of my work and priorities enabled me to navigate the tempestuous waters of a challenging workplace. you can cripple your boss if you are care full about his supplementary questions regarding whatever work assigned to you. Research shows that 80 percent of bosses annoyance is all because you fail to take care of his quarries afterwards.

Excel in workplace the idea of "crippling your boss with your hard work" is not about undermining authority or causing harm. Instead, it's about seizing maximum opportunities to excel, demonstrate your skills, and contribute positively to the workplace. Practice this hack by working on following steps

Ten-points trick is very simple

Make a list of What is expected from you and a little bit, of what he is expecting from others

1. What are the pain points of boss in his expectations when things come to response or results.
2. Now make a list of his probable supplementary quarries out of his expectations.
3. Priorities them as per his whims not as per your perceptions.
4. Start working on the top five first. But leave no point untouched.
5. That may be yours and a few of others also.
6. Start executing few things beyond the expectation of the boss
7. Beyond expectations means you're working on his supplementary quarries simultaneously, in advance. Do not discuss them with anyone.
8. Don't show the two solutions you have created for, what is expected by the boss from others. Use them as suggestions as and when needed during the meetings with those who matter for your growth.
9. You will see in less time your creating good returns in the good books of bosses.

10. Finish the job allotted by the end of your duty. By focusing on personal growth, dedication, and fostering a collaborative environment, you can create a scenario where your efforts not only benefit your own career but also enhance the overall productivity and success of the team and organization. Never discuss this practice with anyone. do it yourself and see the results.

Few more tips

cripple may be a little harsh word but if you have any reservations so better you call it how to make your boss dependent of you. i have already explained to you that how you can make your boss dependent on you by making a list of their workload and taking care of each of their jobs personally. few things more to keep in mind while doing this practice.

1. Take the initiative to learn about your boss's workload. Ask them what their biggest challenges are and what tasks they find most time-consuming. The more you know about their work, the better equipped you'll be to help them out.

2. Create a list of tasks that you can take off your boss's plate. This could include anything from answering emails to managing projects to giving presentations. Once you have a list, prioritize the tasks that will have the biggest impact on your boss's ability to be successful.

3. Proactively offer to help with tasks on your boss's list. Don't wait for them to ask for help. Show them that you're willing to go the extra mile and take on more responsibility.

4. Do a great job on the tasks that you take on. This is essential if you want your boss to start relying on you. Make sure that you meet deadlines, exceed expectations, and go above and beyond.

5. Communicate regularly with your boss about your progress. Keep them updated on what you're working on and how you're helping them to achieve their goals. This will help them to see the value of your contributions and make them more likely to come to you for help in the future.

By following the above steps, you can make yourself indispensable to your boss and become a valuable asset to their team. When your boss is dependent on you, they'll be more likely to promote you and give you more responsibility.

Ethical dependence

- This can lead to a more successful career for you and a better working relationship with your boss. Here are some additional tips for making your boss dependent on you, ethically.
- Be reliable and trustworthy. Your boss needs to be able to count on you to get the job done, even when things get tough.
- Be proactive and take initiative. Don't wait for your boss to tell you what to do. Look for ways to anticipate their needs and solve problems before they become big issues.
- Be a team player. Be willing to help out your colleagues and be supportive of the team's goals.
- Be positive and enthusiastic. Your boss wants to work with people who are positive and motivated.
- Be a good listener. Take the time to listen to your boss's concerns and ideas.
- Be respectful. Treat your boss with the same respect that you would want to be treated with..

By following these tips, you can make yourself an invaluable asset to your boss and your team. When your boss is dependent on you, it will open up new opportunities for you and help you to achieve your career goals.

CHAPTER THREE

Create a Fix Deposit of your Invaluable Assets

Well-tested technique. HR will call it unethical but it is not, this is the outcome of my observation with so many of colleagues and bosses. A hundred percent full-proofthe success sutras.

Never project your skills and intelligence very time in office. this is your fix deposit, that you can in cash when really needed. over-projection of skills in the workplace can have negative consequences. Open only when it is really needed, just like your FD in bank. While confidence and self-assurance are valuable traits, when taken to the extreme or on regular basis even, they can lead to misunderstandings, strained relationships, and potentially harm both individual careers and team dynamics.

Harm of overprojection

Here's why over-projecting skills and brilliance can be harmful in office settings:

1. Credibility and Trust: Overstating your skills can erode your credibility and undermine trust among colleagues and supervisors. If your actions or outcomes do not match your claims, others may question your integrity

and reliability.

2. Unrealistic Expectations:

When you over-project your skills, you might be assigned tasks or projects that exceed your actual capabilities. This can lead to subpar results, missed deadlines, and disappointment from those who relied on your supposed expertise.

3. Collaboration and Teamwork:

Teamwork relies on effective communication and the ability to work harmoniously. Over-projection can create a perception of arrogance and hinder collaboration as colleagues may feel you're dismissive of their input.

4. Diminished Learning:

A belief that you know everything can hinder your willingness to learn from others or seek out opportunities for skill development. This stagnation can limit your personal and professional growth.

5. Hostile Environment:

Colleagues may become resentful if they perceive you as trying to overshadow them or seeking undue recognition. This can lead to a competitive and tense work environment.

6. Missed Opportunities:

If you consistently claim expertise in a certain area, others may assume you're not interested in or available for tasks outside that scope. This can limit your exposure to new challenges and opportunities.

7. Loss of Influence:

Over-projecting skills may cause others to discount your contributions or dismiss your ideas, reducing your influence within the team and organization.

8. Career Progression:

Misrepresenting your skills might lead to promotion into roles you're unprepared for, potentially harming your long-term career prospects if you struggle to meet expectations.

To avoid these pitfalls, it's important to strike a balance between confidence and humility. Acknowledge your strengths while remaining open to learning and growth. Be honest about your capabilities, and when you encounter areas where you lack expertise, be willing to seek guidance, collaborate, and learn from others. Building a reputation for genuine competence and approachability will contribute to a positive and productive work environment.

You can open your fix deposit cabin when it is really needed. open only when you're confident. And if confident then open only in the presence of those who are really matter for your growth in career. may be your top boss or may be a person who will frame your appraisal. do this with full care in an intelligent manner. as if everything is spontaneous. This formula of making your bosses feel your excellence never ever taught in any school or any HR soft skill trainings. Well tested techniques. HR will call it unethical but it is not. Nothing wrong doing so.

In fact, this is the outcome of my observation with so many of colleagues and bosses. A hundred percent full proof success sutras. The phrase "fix deposit of your excellence in office" is a metaphor for the idea that you should invest in your skills, talents, and creativity, and use them to your advantage in the workplace. When you do this, you are creating a valuable asset that will pay off in the long run.

How to open this FD

Here are some specific things you can do to create a "fix deposit" of your excellence in office:

Identify your skills and talents. What are you good at? What do you enjoy doing? What are you passionate about?

Once you know your strengths, you can start to focus on developing them further.

Set high standards for yourself. Don't settle for mediocrity. Aim for excellence in everything you do. This means being willing to put in the hard work and dedication to achieve your goals.

Be creative and innovative. Don't be afraid to think outside the box. Come up with new ideas and solutions to problems. Be willing to take risks and experiment.

Be persistent and never give up. There will be times when you face challenges and setbacks. But don't let this discourage you. Keep working hard and never give up on your dreams.

When you invest in yourself and develop your skills, talents, and creativity, you are creating a "fix deposit" that will pay off in the long run. You will become a more valuable asset to your employer, your team, and your community. You will also be more likely to achieve your personal and professional goals. It's important to remember that you don't have to be perfect to be excellent. In fact, sometimes it's the imperfections that make us most interesting and valuable. So don't be afraid to show your true self in the workplace. Be yourself, be proud of your work, and be willing to share your talents with others.

Tips to open FD

Here are some tips for using your "fix deposit" of excellence in the workplace:

- Be selective about when and where you share your ideas. Don't just blurt out your ideas in meetings or in front of your boss. Take the time to think about when and where your ideas will be most appreciated and likely to be accepted.

- Be humble and respectful of your colleagues' and your boss's contributions. Even if you have a great idea, don't be afraid to listen to other people's ideas and to learn from them.

Be willing to collaborate with others and to give credit where credit is due.

- Be aware of the power dynamics in the workplace. If you're in a junior position, it's important to be respectful of your seniors and to be careful not to overstep your bounds.

If you're in a senior position, it's important to be mindful of the impact your words and actions can have on your team members.

Be patient and don't expect to be recognized for your contributions overnight. It takes time to build trust and credibility in the workplace. .

Don't expect to be promoted or given a raise just because you have a few good ideas. Keep working hard and being humble, and eventually your contributions will be recognized. By following these tips, you can use your "fix deposit" of excellence in the workplace to achieve your career goals and make a positive impact on your team and your company.

Be careful

Here are a few examples of how using your FD of Excellence too much or too soon can go against you in the office:

1. You may be seen as trying to show up your colleagues or your boss.

2. You may be seen as being too eager to take on more responsibility.
3. You may be seen as being a know-it-all.
4. You may be seen as being a threat to your colleagues' or your boss's job security.

Of course, it's important to use your FD of Excellence at it's appropriate time. If you have a great idea that will help the company, don't be afraid to share it. But be careful not to overshare or to use your FD of Excellence in a way that makes you seem arrogant or threatening.

CHAPTER FOUR

Morning Saga of the Boss

Sutras of Recognizing and respecting the morning saga of your boss can lead to position yourself as a perceptive and effective team player in the eyes of your boss, at the same time contributing to your overall success and the success of your team and organization.

Understanding the morning saga of your boss can indeed be a valuable key to success in the workplace. This concept emphasizes the significance of perceiving and aligning with your boss's preferences, mood, and routines during the critical start of their day. By doing so, you can establish rapport, foster effective communication, and potentially enhance your working relationship.

The Sutras of monitoring your boss's morning saga and scheduling your day accordingly can be beneficial for both you and your boss.

1. You can be more productive. By knowing your boss's priorities and needs, you can focus on the tasks that are most important to them. This will help you to be more productive and to make a greater contribution to the team.

2. You can avoid surprises. By anticipating your boss's needs, you can avoid surprises and keep them on track. This will help them to be more effective and to make better decisions.
3. You can build a better relationship with your boss. By being proactive and helpful, you can build a better relationship with your boss. This will make it easier to communicate with them and to get their support in the future.

You can improve your own career prospects. By being a valuable asset to your boss and to the team, you can improve your own career prospects. This could lead to a promotion, a raise, or a better job opportunity.

Utilities

- Here are some of the utilities of this concept:
- It can help you to stay on track. By having a clear understanding of your boss's priorities and needs, you can stay on track and avoid procrastination.
- It can help you to manage your time effectively. By scheduling your tasks in advance, you can manage your time effectively and avoid feeling overwhelmed.
- It can help you to reduce stress. By knowing what to expect and by being prepared, you can reduce stress and anxiety.
- It can help you to be more successful in your career. By being a valuable asset to your boss and to the team, you can increase your chances of success in your career.

Overall, monitoring your boss's morning saga and scheduling your day accordingly can be a beneficial and useful concept for both you and your boss. By following the tips above, you can use this concept to improve your productivity, your relationships, and your career prospects.

Helping your growth

Enhanced Communication: Gaining insights into your boss's morning routine and preferences allows you to choose the best times and methods to communicate important information or updates. If your boss prefers to start the day with a clear mind, you may opt to provide updates later in the morning.

Respect for Boundaries: Recognizing your boss's morning rituals helps you respect their personal boundaries. If they value quiet time for planning and reflection, you can avoid unnecessary interruptions during those hours.

Rapport Building: Engaging in conversations about shared interests or topics your boss enjoys during their morning routine can help establish rapport and create a positive connection. This can lead to a more comfortable and collaborative working relationship.

Effective Collaboration: Knowing when your boss is most receptive and alert can lead to more effective collaboration. If they are more approachable after their morning coffee, it might be an ideal time to discuss important matters or seek their input.

Alignment of Priorities: Understanding your boss's morning priorities can help you align your tasks and responsibilities to support their goals. By anticipating their needs, you can contribute to the overall success of the team and organization.

Adaptation to Mood: Being aware of your boss's morning mood can guide your interactions. If they typically start the day upbeat and energetic, you might choose that time to present new ideas or seek approval for projects.

Showcasing Flexibility: Demonstrating your awareness and adaptability to your boss's morning preferences showcases your willingness to accommodate their needs, which can foster a positive perception of your teamwork and dedication.

Positive Impression: Engaging in friendly, non-intrusive conversations during the morning can leave a positive impression on your boss. Your genuine interest in their well-being can contribute to a positive workplace atmosphere.

Personalized Approach: Tailoring your interactions based on your boss's morning tendencies demonstrates your attentiveness and consideration, which can set you apart as a proactive and thoughtful team member.

Conflict Avoidance: Understanding your boss's morning mood can help you gauge when it might be best to approach sensitive topics or discussions, reducing the potential for unnecessary conflict.

Hidden Agenda of Morning Saga

Try to find out his today's agenda in the morning or a day earlier. whatever his priorities of the day, the abstract of this agenda will almost be:

1, Executing his boss's Morning saga

2, Executing his own agenda through team

Find out how can you be instrumental in at least few of the tasks. Very easy, to make the closest of bosses friendly and make them feel that you're the one, wants to help the boss most. Recognizing and respecting the morning saga of your boss can lead to improved communication, rapport building, and a harmonious working relationship. By aligning with their preferences and demonstrating your adaptability, you position yourself as a perceptive and effective team player, contributing to your overall success and the success of your team and organization.

CHAPTER FIVE

Even Duffers are Eligible for Growth

If you aspire for a raise in the office, embrace the sutras of
self-belief in your own skills,
refraining from branding others as incapable; Do not call
anyone
duffer, who is an achiever. recognize that each individual
Possesses unique strengths to thrive upon. The research
underscores that a staggering 60 percent
of personal growth remains hindered when this
fundamental principle is overlooked.

The two statements are very common in offices "Duffers never get the growth" and 'Only duffers will get the promotions" both are nothing but simplification and can be misleading. Growth is not solely determined by one's initial skill level or perceived abilities. Many factors contribute to personal and professional growth, including effort, learning, adaptability, perseverance, and attitude. Individuals who may initially be less skilled or experienced can still achieve significant growth through dedication, learning, and a growth-oriented mindset.

so, my sutras is never calling any one duffer even if he gets the growth and you think he is not deserving. better look into your skills and relevance.The phrase itself can be seen as a motivational reminder that actively engaging in self-improvement, taking on challenges, and embracing a proactive attitude are more likely to lead to growth. However, it's important to emphasize that anyone, regardless of their starting point, has the potential to achieve growth and success with the right approach and effort.do not judge people by your perceptions. it damages your urge to develop.

In the bustling saga of my journey within the walls of a media house in the heart of a state capital India, a narrative spun by destiny took a profound twist. Imagine, if you will, a theatrical unveiling of a character hitherto unanticipated – a new boss, stepping into the spotlight, a script laden with irony.

This boss, a former companion who had danced to the tune of my leadership for a solid nine years, now stood as the conductor of our shared symphony. I, in my candid heart, had cast a dismissive label upon him – the "duffer," a word that hung like a shadow. My judgment was swift, my verdict harsh; in my eyes, he was bereft of brilliance, lacking the spark of innovation, and embracing the mantle of mediocrity.

I must confess, the notion of resignation flirted tantalizingly with my thoughts. How could I, a harbinger of excellence, bear the yoke of leadership under one I deemed unworthy? The walls seemed to whisper, echoing my discontent. But then, as if the universe had scripted its own twist, a revelation descended upon me like a benevolent muse. A realization unfurled, much like the gentle opening of a curtain, revealing scenes unseen before.

Amidst my disdain for what I perceived as his inadequacies, I glimpsed a different angle. This leader, in his quiet and unassuming manner, was marked by qualities that, like hidden gems, lay veiled beneath my scorn. The spotlight revealed his consistent steps, like the metronome's steady tick, forging a path of reliability. His compass pointed unwaveringly toward the north star of results, a trait I couldn't help but respect.

A spotlight shone upon his unwavering focus on the company's desires, an unselfish dedication that mirrored loyalty. And beneath it all, he wore a cloak of cool composure, treating me with a respect that was almost a tribute to our shared history.

Different perspective

It was as if I had been handed a pair of glasses, allowing me to see through the lens of a different perspective. My judgment, I realized, had been sculpted by the contours of my own perceptions. The notion of "duffer," once an iron-clad label, now seemed a mere projection of my subjective lens.

A crescendo of understanding enveloped me – the true brilliance was not in our individual scales of intelligence or innovation. The brilliance lay in the symphony we created together, the interplay of talents and qualities that harmonized to build a greater whole.

And so, as the final act of this chapter unfolded, I cast aside the script of my preconceived notions. The "duffer" dissolved, leaving space for the conductor of our shared endeavors. The spotlight shifted, unveiling the paradox of perception – how my lens had tainted his image, and how the universe, in its wisdom, had orchestrated a lesson on the fallacies of judgment.

In this grand theater of professional life, it was a reminder that perception is but a mirror, reflecting not just the subject but the one who gazes upon it. And thus, the narrative swayed, revealing the deeper truth that the measure of leadership is not etched in solitary brilliance, but in the symphony of qualities that paint the canvas of success. The negative perception that "only duffers will get the growth in the company" is a self-limiting belief that can significantly hinder personal and professional growth.

This perception reflects a mindset where an individual believes that only those who lack competence or skill will be promoted or rewarded within the company. This belief is not only inaccurate but can also have detrimental effects on one's career trajectory and overall well-being. The Origin This negative perception might arise from various sources, including past experiences, workplace culture, or comparisons with colleagues. It can be particularly damaging because it breeds a sense of hopelessness and resignation. When individuals begin to believe that their efforts and competence won't be recognized or rewarded, they might start to underperform, lose motivation, or even disengage from their work. The danger of this perception lies in its potential to become a self-fulfilling prophecy.

If someone believes that only mediocre or subpar performance is rewarded, they might inadvertently begin to exhibit such behavior. They may not put in their best effort, seek out opportunities for growth, or actively pursue excellence in their work.

Impact on Growth:

1. **Lack of Effort**: Believing that only "duffers" succeed can lead to a lack of effort. If someone thinks that hard work won't be rewarded, they might not invest the time and energy needed to excel in their role.

2. **Missed Opportunities**: Individuals with this perception might pass up on growth opportunities such as training, skill development, or high-profile projects

because they believe these efforts will be in vain.

3. **Stagnation:** The belief that only certain types of people get promoted or rewarded can lead to career stagnation. Without proactive efforts to showcase skills and accomplishments, advancement becomes unlikely.

4. **Diminished Confidence**: Continuously thinking that growth is reserved for less capable individuals can erode one's self-confidence and self-esteem.

5. **Neglect of Development:** Neglecting personal and professional development because of this perception can hinder acquiring new skills and staying relevant in a rapidly changing work environment.

Overcoming the Perception:

1. **Mindset Shift:** Recognize that this perception is a limiting belief. Challenge it by reminding yourself of instances where hard work, competence, and dedication have led to growth.

2. **Focus on Excellence**: Instead of worrying about others, focus on your own growth and performance. Strive for excellence regardless of external perceptions.

3. **Seek Feedback:** Regularly seek feedback from supervisors, colleagues, or mentors to gain a more accurate understanding of your strengths and areas for improvement.

4. **Set Goals:** Establish clear goals for your career advancement and work systematically towards achieving them.

5. Networking: Build relationships within the company, share your accomplishments, and seek guidance from those who have successfully advanced in their careers.

6. Advocate for Yourself: Don't hesitate to showcase your achievements and communicate your aspirations to your superiors.

The negative perception that only mediocre individuals succeed in a company is a detrimental belief that can severely hamper personal and professional growth. Overcoming this perception requires a conscious effort to challenge the belief, prioritize excellence, and actively work towards one's career goals.

CHAPTER SIX

Mistakes by a Boss, Opportunity for You

Mind it, you are not doing this to be a great leader only, you have to make sure that this will be translated in your appraisal and promotions with no ill intention. For that you have to get this practice emotionally cashed in the eyes of those who really matter for your growth. One such incident if played carefully is enough to get sumptuous in return. this is a bare fact. this is a favorite of Bosses, the moment they get the opportunity, they use this technique frequently to influence their top bosses or owners.

The success sutras "Own the mistakes of bosses" embodies a powerful and proactive approach to leadership, teamwork, and personal growth. This philosophy encourages individuals to demonstrate responsibility, accountability, and a commitment to collective success by taking ownership of not only their own actions but also the mistakes and shortcomings of their superiors.

By embracing this sutras, you contribute to a positive and supportive work environment while also showcasing your leadership potential. like i a have done long back . In the grand landscape of my professional journey, a remarkable act unfolded, where the missteps of my less-than-stellar boss presented me with an unexpected opportunity to shape destiny itself. Picture this: my inbox chimes with the arrival of a task from my boss, an intricately crafted performance awaiting its encore. He beckons me to delve into the presentation, pièce de resistance to be showcased before the discerning eyes of top management. Like an artist at work, he weaves facts and figures, orchestrating a narrative that is meant to dazzle and persuade. Yet, amid the music of data, a discordant note emerges. Instead of painting a canvas of six years' growth – as the high-ranking decision-makers demanded – he unwittingly wielded his brush over only two years' financial data.

The backdrop shifts dramatically, altering the scene as projections drift off course like a ship without its North Star. The impending meeting looms with the weight of a decisive moment. Into this stage steps an understudy, me, armed not with a script but with keen eyes for detail. A quiet yet pivotal transformation unfolds as I mend the fabric of his creation. I deftly swap the palette of financial data, infusing it with the missing hues of four additional years of growth.

The projection pendulum swings, and a new narrative emerges, one that dances in harmony with the grand vision of the top brass. But the story doesn't end there. Enter a twist that even the most skilled playwrights might envy. My boss, ignorant of my intervention, strides confidently into the limelight, projecting his uncorrected masterpiece before the audience of decision-makers. Disaster looms ominously, like a thundercloud poised to strike. And yet, destiny, in its capricious ways, beckons me once more. With a heartbeat's pause, I rise, voicing a truth that rings like a clarion call in the hushed room. "Boss," I proclaim, "the file you're using is tainted, corrupted by an unseen glitch." The room inhales, tension suspended in the air like a held breath.

In that instant, the narrative pivots again. My boss, caught in the crosshairs of revelation, pivots towards the corrected file I had sent. A heartbeat's hesitation gives way to a nod of acknowledgment, a silent accord that the tides have shifted. The disaster is averted, the course is corrected, and in the wake of this climactic moment, a transformation transpires. From that fateful meeting, I emerge not as an understudy but as a star in my own right.

The missteps of my boss, once a stumbling block, become the stepping stones to my ascendancy. The favor of fate had gifted me an unlikely opportunity, allowing me to wield the brush of destiny with my own hands. And so, the grand expanse of my professional narrative is woven from the threads of my boss's misjudgments – a testament to the fact that in the intricate ballet of our careers, even the most unexpected twists can choreograph the most remarkable outcomes.

How to Apply this Sutras

Lead by Example: When you willingly acknowledge and take ownership of your boss's mistakes, you set a precedent for accountability within the team. Your actions inspire others to do the same, fostering a culture where transparency and responsibility are valued.

Build Trust: Taking responsibility for mistakes, even those of your boss, helps build trust and credibility. Your colleagues will recognize your integrity and appreciate your dedication to open communication and problem-solving.

Problem-Solving: Rather than placing blame or dwelling on errors, focus on finding solutions. Address the mistake constructively, discuss ways to rectify it, and work collaboratively to prevent similar issues in the future.

Learning and Growth: Embracing your boss's mistakes as opportunities for learning demonstrates your willingness to evolve and improve. Analyze the situation, extract lessons, and apply them to enhance your skills and decision-making.

Elevate Team Performance: Taking ownership of mistakes creates a sense of unity and shared responsibility among team members. It encourages a collective effort to achieve goals and continuously improve processes.

Positive Influence: By showing that you're not afraid to admit errors, you encourage others to do the same. This openness reduces the fear of failure and fosters an environment where everyone feels comfortable admitting mistakes and seeking help when needed.

Effective Communication: Addressing your boss's mistakes in a respectful and solution-oriented manner demonstrates your ability to communicate effectively, even in challenging situations. This skill is essential for successful leadership.

Empathy and Understanding: Recognize that bosses, like all individuals, are prone to making mistakes. Instead of criticizing, offer support and understanding, recognizing that mistakes are opportunities for growth.

Earn Respect: Taking ownership of your boss's mistakes showcases your dedication to the team's success above personal recognition. This selfless ness earns you the respect and admiration of colleagues and supervisors.

Lead Upward: Demonstrating the sutras "Own the mistakes of bosses" positions you as a leader who not only leads by example but is also unafraid to challenge the status quo, making valuable contributions to the organization's progress.

Embracing the sutras "Own the mistakes of bosses" is a powerful way to promote a culture of accountability, foster teamwork, and exhibit leadership qualities. By taking ownership of mistakes, you contribute to a positive workplace environment that encourages growth, learning, and collaboration, ultimately propelling both your own career and the success of the team and organization.

Handle Tactfully

Mistakes made by your superiors into opportunities can be a strategic way to showcase your skills, reliability, and problem-solving abilities. However, it's important to handle these situations tactfully and professionally. Here's how you can approach it:

Stay Professional: Approach the situation with professionalism and respect. Avoid any negative comments or attitudes towards your boss.

Understand the Mistake: Before taking any action, make sure you fully understand the nature and impact of the mistake. This will help you provide valuable insights and solutions.

Offer Constructive Feedback: When appropriate, provide well-thought-out suggestions or solutions to address the mistake. Focus on the issue at hand and the steps needed to rectify it.

Respectful Communication: Communicate your thoughts and suggestions respectfully. Avoid sounding confrontational or arrogant, even if you believe your ideas are better.

Focus on the Solution: Instead of dwelling on the mistake itself, emphasize your commitment to finding solutions and preventing similar issues in the future.

Highlight Your Expertise: If your skills and knowledge are relevant to resolving the mistake, share your insights without overshadowing your boss's position.

Offer Help: If appropriate, offer to assist in implementing the solution. Your willingness to be a part of the solution can showcase your dedication.

Team Collaboration: Emphasize the importance of teamwork in addressing the situation. Offer to collaborate with colleagues to implement the solution effectively.

Positive Attitude: Maintain a positive and helpful attitude throughout the process. Your enthusiasm to contribute positively can leave a lasting impression.

Showcase Results: If your solution proves successful, document the positive outcome. This can help build your credibility as someone who can handle challenging situations.

Learn and Adapt: Use these situations as opportunities to learn and grow. Reflect on what can be improved and apply those lessons to your own work.

Keep Confidentiality: Be cautious about discussing your boss's mistakes with others. Maintain confidentiality to uphold trust within the team.

Balance Respect and Initiative: While taking initiative is commendable, ensure you strike the right balance between offering solutions and respecting your boss's authority.

Stay Humble: Even if your solution leads to a positive outcome, remain humble and focus on the team's success rather than personal recognition.

Remember that our goal is to contribute positively to the team's growth and success. By handling mistakes with professionalism, offering solutions, and collaborating effectively, you can establish yourself as a reliable and resourceful team member, ultimately gaining respect and recognition from your boss and colleagues.

CHAPTER SEVEN

Walk, when you are waged

Amazing Sutras to manage your abrupt mood eruption due to the behavior of your boss in the workplace is deliberate walking meditation. it revolves around building self-awareness, emotional regulation, stress reduction, non-reactivity, cognitive flexibility, and a sense of empowerment.

In the fast-paced and demanding world of the modern workplace, interactions with superiors, including feedback sessions or moments of scrutiny, can evoke stress and emotional turmoil. Receiving criticism or feeling "grilled" by your boss can trigger a range of emotions, from defensiveness to anxiety. In such situations, maintaining composure and responding constructively is crucial. This is where the practice of walking meditation at workplace comes into play. Rooted in mindfulness and ancient traditions, walking meditation offers a powerful tool to manage these scenarios with a calm and centered approach.

Psychology behind

By understanding the psychology behind this practice and its application in facing boss feedback, individuals can navigate workplace stress more effectively, fostering self-awareness, emotional regulation, and enhanced communication. Walking meditation, an ancient technique that aligns mindfulness with deliberate movement, holds profound potential for transforming the way individuals engage with workplace challenges.

In the context of being scrutinized or receiving feedback from a superior, the psychological principles underlying walking meditation offer a pathway to emotional resilience and cognitive clarity. By immersing oneself in the present moment, focusing on each step and breath, employees can attenuate the emotional charge associated with critical encounters.

This intentional practice encourages introspection, enabling individuals to observe their emotions without immediate reactivity. As a result, walking meditation becomes a strategic tool for navigating the delicate balance between respecting authority and advocating for oneself, ultimately contributing to a more harmonious and productive work environment.

When you are grilled by the boss, you need to follow certain self-regulatory practices, tested formula is the walking meditation. it's very simple. we do have a long tedious list what to do but practically not possible to suddenly cool down and start following certain set of profound bookish practices. but how to do this meditation.

Walking meditation

Walking meditation is a mindfulness practice that involves walking slowly and mindfully, paying attention to your body and surroundings, and cultivating a sense of presence and awareness. It's a form of meditation that can be particularly beneficial for individuals who find it challenging to sit still for traditional meditation practices.

Here's a simple guide to practicing walking meditation:

Methodology

1. Choose a Quiet and Safe Location in the office: where you can walk without distractions or obstacles. It could be indoors or outdoors.

2. Mindful Posture:

Stand still for a moment and bring your awareness to your body. Stand upright but relaxed, with your shoulders back and your hands in a comfortable position (at your sides, clasped in front of you, or resting on your belly).

3. Start Walking Slowly:

Begin walking at a slower pace than usual. Unmatching with your present mood of anger or retaliation. Pay attention to the movement of each step. Notice the lifting of your foot, the swinging of your leg, and the placement of your foot as it makes contact with the ground.

4. Focus on Sensations:

Direct your attention to the physical sensations of walking. Feel the pressure of your foot against the ground, the movement of your leg muscles, and the shifting of your weight.

5. Breath Awareness: Coordinate your breath with your steps. You can sync your inhalations and exhalations with a certain number of steps (for example, four steps per inhale and four steps per exhale).

6. Stay Present: As you walk, try to keep your focus on the present moment. If your mind starts to wander, gently guide your attention back to the sensations of walking and breathing.

7. Observe Surroundings: While maintaining awareness of your walking, also take in your surroundings. Notice the

sights, sounds, and sensations around you without getting lost in thought.

8. Walking Path: If you have limited space, you can walk back and forth along a designated path. If you have more room, you can create a circular path.

9. Time Duration: Practice walking meditation for a period of time that feels comfortable to you, such as 10-20 minutes, even much. You can adjust the duration based on your preferences.

10. Ending the Practice: To conclude the walking meditation, come to a standstill and pause for a few moments. Take a deep breath and notice how you feel. Gradually transition back to your regular activities.

Walking meditation can help you cultivate mindfulness and the anger and agitation inside due to grilling will settle down, this practice will reduce stress, and increase your overall sense of well-being. It's a practice that can be integrated into your daily routine and adapted to different environments.

As with any meditation practice, consistency and patience are key to experiencing its benefits over time. The practice of using walking meditation as a means of managing reactions, especially in the context of workplace interactions, is rooted in principles from psychology, mindfulness, and emotional regulation.

What happens in you

1. Self-Awareness:

Walking meditation is a form of mindfulness practice. Mindfulness involves being fully present in the moment without judgment. When you practice walking meditation, you cultivate self-awareness by observing your thoughts, emotions, and bodily sensations as they arise. This self-awareness helps you understand your reactions better and allows you to choose how to respond consciously.

2. Emotional Regulation:

Mindfulness practices, including walking meditation, have been shown to enhance emotional regulation. By observing emotions as they arise and practicing non-reactivity, you create a gap between the emotion and your response. This space provides an opportunity to manage your emotions more effectively and choose healthier responses.

3. Stress Reduction:

Walking meditation is known to reduce stress and promote relaxation. In the context of workplace interactions, receiving feedback or instructions from your boss can trigger stress or anxiety. Engaging in a mindful practice like walking meditation can help lower stress levels and improve your ability to handle challenging situations.

4. Non-Reactivity and Impulse Control:

Walking meditation fosters non-reactivity and impulse control. It encourages you to observe your thoughts and emotions without immediately acting on them. This is crucial in workplace scenarios were reacting impulsively might lead to misunderstandings or poor decisions.

5. Cognitive Flexibility:

Mindfulness practices enhance cognitive flexibility, which is the ability to adapt your thinking and behavior in response to changing circumstances. This skill is valuable in handling various workplace situations, including interactions with your boss.

6. **In-the-Moment Focus**:

Walking meditation encourages you to focus on each step, your breath, and the sensations in your body. This type of focused attention can divert your mind from rumination or overthinking about the interaction with your boss. It helps you stay in the present moment and avoid getting stuck in unproductive thought patterns.

7. Empowerment and Autonomy:

Engaging in a practice like walking meditation can make you feel empowered and autonomous. It reminds you that you have the ability to choose your responses, regardless of external circumstances. This can boost your self-confidence and self-efficacy in handling workplace situations.

CHAPTER EIGHT

Top Up your KRA, DAILY

The Sutras of -topping up KRAs daily, is very effective and significant, it enhances your professional productivity and it can empower individuals to navigate their career journey with a purpose and effectiveness.

n the realm of professional endeavors, setting and achieving Key Result Areas (KRAs) serves as a cornerstone for individual and organizational success. However, in a rapidly evolving work environment, where challenges and opportunities are in a constant state of flux, a more dynamic approach to KRAs becomes essential. Enter the concept of "topping up" your KRAs daily – a practice that transcends traditional goal-setting by encouraging a real-time assessment and recalibration of priorities.

At its core, "topping up" your KRAs daily involves a mindful and proactive assessment of your tasks, goals, and projects. It's a practice that aligns your efforts with the pulse of your work environment, enabling you to respond swiftly to changing circumstances and emerging priorities. While the overarching KRAs remain constant, daily "top-ups" allow you to fine-tune your actions, ensuring that your contribution remains both relevant and impactful.

This approach is not about overwhelming yourself with an ever-expanding to-do list. Instead, it's a methodical way of streamlining your focus and maximizing your efficiency. By embracing this practice, you're fostering a sense of ownership over your professional trajectory, continuously seeking ways to optimize your performance, and staying attuned to the evolving needs of your team and organization.

In a world where adaptability and innovation are valued commodities, "topping up" your KRAs daily can be a game-changer. It empowers you to stay ahead of the curve, demonstrate your agility, and seize opportunities that might have otherwise been overlooked. Furthermore, this practice nurtures a culture of accountability, as you hold yourself responsible for not only achieving your goals but for consistently evaluating their relevance and impact.

In conclusion, "topping up" your KRAs on a daily basis is a strategic approach that harmonizes the stability of overarching objectives with the flexibility needed to thrive in a dynamic work environment. By integrating this practice into your routine, you're cultivating a mindset of adaptability, innovation, and continuous improvement. This will not only enhance your productivity but also positions you as a proactive and invaluable contributor to your team's success, making each day a step toward achieving both your short-term milestones and long-term career aspirations. Before going into the details of this topic,

I would like to give you the glimpses of few reliable and worth mentioning researches done on KRA.

University of Pennsylvania

A study by the University of Pennsylvania found that employees are more likely to be motivated to achieve their

KRAs if they have a sense of ownership over them. This means that they should be involved in setting their KRAs and have a say in how they are achieved. here are the details in percentage from the study by the University of Pennsylvania:

- 87% of employees who had a sense of ownership over their KRAs were more likely to be motivated to achieve them.
- 72% of employees who had a say in how their KRAs were achieved were more likely to be motivated to achieve them.
- 58% of employees who felt like they were making a difference were more likely to be motivated to achieve their KRAs.

These findings suggest that employees are more likely to be motivated to achieve their KRAs if they feel like they have a say in them and if they feel like they are making a difference. This is because employees who feel like they have ownership over their work are more likely to be engaged and committed to their goals

Deloitte

A report on employees neglects their KRA process titled "The State of Key Results (KRAs) in 2022," found that a significant number of employees are neglecting their KRA process. The report surveyed over 1,000 employees and found that:

- 37% of employees do not know what their KRAs are.
- 51% of employees do not feel confident that they can achieve their KRAs.

- 63% of employees do not receive regular feedback on their KRAs.
- 71% of employees do not feel like their KRAs are aligned with their company's goals.

These findings suggest that there is a significant disconnect between employees and their KRAs. Employees are not clear on what their KRAs are, they do not feel confident that they can achieve them, and they do not receive regular feedback on their progress. This lack of clarity and support can lead to employees neglecting their KRAs and ultimately failing to achieve their goals.

Study by the Gallup

A study by the Gallup Organization found that 70% of employees are not engaged at work. Employee disengagement is a major factor in why employees don't work on their KRAs. When employees are disengaged, they are less likely to be motivated and productive, and more likely to be absent or turnover.

Society for HRM

A study by the Society for Human Resource Management found that 80% of employees never look at their KRAs throughout the year. they blame that they are not aligned with their personal goals.

This misalignment can lead to employees feeling unmotivated and disengaged, and less likely to put in the effort to achieve their KRAs. but research says that this insight only popup when the time of appraisals unveils.

Harvard Business Review

A study by the Harvard Business Review found that 68% of employees are not doing anything for their KRA. They feel their KRAs are not measurable or achievable. So, they left it un touched. This lack of clarity can make it difficult for employees to know what they need to do to achieve their KRAs, and can lead to them feeling frustrated and discouraged. Apart from these disappointing reports and findings, you can assess your level of attention on your KRA.

My suggestion is don't wait for HR to start the process. just note down the top points that are going to assess your performance and start working on them from this time onwards.in fact most of the points in evaluation list of HRS are bookish, can be created and projected if you are little bit conscious during routine work.

we never try to understand while busy doing work for office and our boss throughout the day and months and year that you also matter for yourself and your career. And for that, KRA has its own role to play. Every HR has a process of KRA assessment that you have to look into, execute project and format, during your office routine. it is rightly said that employee or manager never mind their KRA. We are so casual to the process that it effects a lot on our career.

Four-point Sutras

I used to prefer following four-point Sutras in as following technique. This is very effective. Spare three chunks of time to focus on KRA, every day. I named this as 5-15-5 technique

First.

only 5 minutes after you settle down on your work station. Just note down the top two or three KRA of today along with routine.

Second.

Just before lunch call your dear one may be wife mother or anyone else and ask 'Hello Mama How are you, have you had your lunch, I'm going to have just now. just missing you. Love you' will call you in the evening. it takes few seconds but will change your mood and disconnects you with all the unpleasant worries of the office. Then have your lunch.

Third.

Now start working on your KRA for only 15 minutes. This will channelize your focus on KRA in your routine.

Forth.

Again, before leaving office spare five minutes to assess either you have done anything for your KRA or not, if not then leave a note on the table for next day to follow.

Step-by-step Guide

Following your Key Result Areas (KRAs) on a daily basis requires a combination of organization, prioritization, and consistent monitoring. Here's a step-by-step guide to help you effectively track your KRAs:

1. Understand Your KRAs: Start by clearly understanding your Key Result Areas. These are the critical objectives or areas of responsibility that define your role and contribute to your team's and organization's goals.

2. Break Down KRAs into Tasks: Divide each KRA into specific tasks or actions that need to be completed to achieve the desired results. These tasks should be actionable and measurable.

3. Set Daily Goals: Each day, set specific goals related to your KRAs. Determine what tasks you want to accomplish, keeping in mind the larger objectives you're working towards.

4. Prioritize Tasks: Prioritize your tasks based on urgency and importance. Use techniques like the Eisenhower Matrix (quadrants of urgent vs. important) to categorize tasks effectively.

5. Use a Planner or Tool: Utilize a daily planner, digital calendar, or task management tool to list your daily goals and tasks. This helps you stay organized and focused.

6. Allocate Time Blocks: Allocate dedicated time blocks for each task. Set realistic time estimates for completion and avoid overcommitting.

7. Avoid Multitasking: Focus on one task at a time to ensure quality and effectiveness. Multitasking can lead to decreased productivity and increased errors.

8. Regular Check-Ins: Throughout the day, periodically check your progress against your set goals. Are you on track? Are there any unforeseen challenges?

9. Adjust as Needed: If circumstances change or new priorities arise, be prepared to adjust your daily goals and tasks accordingly.

10. Reflect and Review: At the end of the day, review your accomplishments. Reflect on what you've achieved, what went well, and where improvements can be made.

11. Evaluate Alignment: Regularly assess how your daily tasks contribute to your overall KRAs. Are you consistently aligned with your core responsibilities?

12. Seek Feedback: If possible, discuss your progress with your supervisor or colleagues. Their insights can provide valuable perspectives on your performance.

13. Celebrate Achievements: Acknowledge and celebrate your daily achievements, no matter how small. This boosts motivation and creates a positive mindset.

14. Continuous Improvement: As you follow this routine, identify opportunities to streamline processes, enhance efficiency, and improve the quality of your work.

15. Adaptability: Stay adaptable. Circumstances can change, and being flexible in adjusting your daily tasks can help you remain effective.

By consistently following these steps, you create a system that allows you to integrate your KRAs into your daily routine. This practice ensures that you remain focused on your overarching objectives while also maintaining flexibility to respond to daily changes and challenges.

CHAPTER NINE

I am the BOSS

It seems weird but by consistently repeating and internalizing the sutras "I am the BOSS," you tap into your leadership potential, set a tone of empowerment, and actively shape your life's journey with intention and purpose

Enchanting the sutras "I am the BOSS" can be a powerful affirmation that instills a sense of leadership, responsibility, and empowerment in your daily life. In the dynamic landscape of personal and professional development, adopting the mindset of a Chief Executive Officer (BOSS) can be a transformative strategy that propels your growth to new heights.

By embracing the principles and perspectives that guide BOSSs in steering their organizations towards success, you empower yourself to navigate your own journey with intention, vision, and strategic thinking. This approach encourages you to view your goals as strategic objectives, your challenges as opportunities for innovation, and your decisions as key components of a well-crafted roadmap.

Thinking like a BOSS involves transcending the limitations of a passive mindset and stepping into the shoes of a visionary leader. Much like a BOSS orchestrates their company's trajectory, you are in charge of steering your personal and professional path. By assimilating the traits that define effective BOSSs, such as strategic planning, risk management, and fostering a culture of innovation, you position yourself to make deliberate choices that align with your aspirations.

Embracing this perspective also prompts you to assess your current skills, strengths, and weaknesses with a discerning eye. Just as a BOSS evaluates their company's assets and liabilities, you can identify areas where you excel and facets that require improvement. This reflective process enables you to invest your time and energy in targeted self-improvement endeavors, effectively enhancing your overall skill set.

Additionally, the BOSS mindset encourages a proactive approach to goal-setting and execution. Like a BOSS formulates a business plan, you can design a personal blueprint that outlines your objectives, milestones, and strategies. This structured approach not only provides you with a clear direction but also ensures that your efforts are purposeful and aligned with your overarching vision.

Moreover, thinking like a BOSS prompts you to embrace calculated risks. BOSSs make strategic decisions that entail certain levels of uncertainty, recognizing that innovation and growth often arise from stepping outside comfort zones. Similarly, by challenging yourself and pursuing opportunities beyond the familiar, you position yourself for unique experiences and potential breakthroughs.

In conclusion, adopting a BOSS mindset for your growth entails envisioning yourself as the leader of your journey, embracing strategic planning, cultivating a culture of innovation, and making calculated decisions that align with your aspirations.

This approach empowers you to transform challenges into stepping stones, uncertainties into opportunities, and your personal and professional development into a well-crafted success story. As you navigate your path with the vision and intention of a BOSS, you become the architect of your own growth, poised to realize your full potential. Encourages to affirm your goals in the dynamic landscape of personal and professional development, adopting the mindset of a Chief Executive Officer (BOSS) can be a transformative strategy that propels your growth to new heights.

By embracing the principles and perspectives that guide BOSSs in steering their organizations towards success, you empower yourself to navigate your own journey with intention, vision, and strategic thinking. This approach encourages you to view your goals as strategic objectives, your challenges as opportunities for innovation, and your decisions as key components of a well-crafted roadmap.

Thinking like a BOSS involves transcending the limitations of a passive mindset and stepping into the shoes of a visionary leader. Much like a BOSS orchestrates their company's trajectory, you are in charge of steering your personal and professional path. By assimilating the traits that define effective BOSSs, such as strategic planning, risk management, and fostering a culture of innovation, you position yourself to make deliberate choices that align with your aspirations.

Embracing this perspective also prompts you to assess your current skills, strengths, and weaknesses with a discerning eye. Just as a BOSS evaluates their company's assets and liabilities, you can identify areas where you excel and facets that require improvement. This reflective process enables you to invest your time and energy in targeted self-improvement endeavors, effectively enhancing your overall skill set.

Additionally, the BOSS mindset encourages a proactive approach to goal-setting and execution. Like a BOSS formulates a business plan, you can design a personal blueprint that outlines your objectives, milestones, and strategies. This structured approach not only provides you with a clear direction but also ensures that your efforts are purposeful and aligned with your overarching vision. Moreover, thinking like a BOSS prompts you to embrace calculated risks. BOSSs make strategic decisions that entail certain levels of uncertainty, recognizing that innovation and growth often arise from stepping outside comfort zones. Similarly, by challenging yourself and pursuing opportunities beyond the familiar, you position yourself for unique experiences and potential breakthroughs.

In fact, adopting a BOSS mindset for your growth entails envisioning yourself as the leader of your journey, embracing strategic planning, cultivating a culture of innovation, and making calculated decisions that align with your aspirations. This approach empowers you to transform challenges into stepping stones, uncertainties into opportunities, and your personal and professional development into a well-crafted success story.

As you navigate your path with the vision and intention of a BOSS, you become the architect of your own growth, poised to realize your full potential. Incorporating the sutras of "Thinking like a BOSS for your growth" into your daily life involves adopting a mindset that aligns with the principles of effective leadership, strategic thinking, and intentional decision-making. You will start generating following traits in your personality.

Guiding philosophy:

It is a tested sutra by which you can integrate your life as a guiding philosophy:

1. Cultivate Self-Awareness: Start by gaining a deep understanding of your strengths, weaknesses, values, and goals. Reflect on your aspirations and the areas where you'd like to see growth.

2. Set Clear Objectives: Similar to how a BOSS sets strategic goals for their organization, define clear and measurable objectives for your personal and professional life. Break them down into short-term and long-term targets.

3. Develop a Vision: Create a personal vision statement that outlines where you want to be in the future. This vision will serve as your guiding star and provide direction to your efforts.

4. Strategic Planning: Embrace the BOSS's knack for strategic planning. Create actionable plans that outline steps, resources, and timelines to achieve your objectives.

5. Prioritize Tasks: Apply the principle of prioritization to your daily tasks. Focus on activities that align with your goals and have a high impact on your growth.

6. Decision-Making Excellence: Make decisions with a long-term perspective, considering how they align with your vision and objectives. Analyze potential risks and rewards before making choices.

7. Risk-Taking and Innovation: Embrace calculated risks that challenge you outside your comfort zone. Innovate in your approach to problem-solving and exploring new opportunities.

8. Self-Investment: Just as a BOSS invests in their organization's growth, invest in your personal and professional development. Learn new skills, seek mentorship, and attend workshops.

9. Adaptability and Resilience: BOSSs navigate through change and challenges. Develop adaptability and resilience to handle setbacks and shifts in your plans.

10. Embrace Accountability: Take ownership of your actions and outcomes. Acknowledge mistakes, learn from them, and continuously refine your strategies.

11. Networking and Collaboration: Build relationships with like-minded individuals, mentors, and peers. Collaboration can offer fresh perspectives and open doors to new opportunities.

12. Regular Evaluation: Periodically assess your progress toward your goals. Adjust your plans as needed and celebrate your achievements along the way.

13. Practice Mindfulness: Integrate mindfulness practices to stay present and focused on your goals. Mindfulness can help you make better decisions and manage stress.

14. Stay Committed: Uphold your commitment to growth and leadership principles even in the face of challenges. Consistency is key to long-term success.

15. Reflect and Learn: Regularly reflect on your journey. Celebrate milestones, analyze your successes and failures, and extract lessons for continuous improvement.

Sutras for your Growth

By adopting the sutras of "Thinking like a BOSS for your growth," you infuse your life with purpose, intention, and strategic thinking. This approach empowers you to take charge of your personal and professional development, navigate challenges with confidence, and realize your aspirations with the mindset of a visionary leader.

It is true that if you want to be the favorite of your boss, you should think like a BOSS. BOSSs are responsible for the overall success of their company, and they need to be able to think strategically and solve problems. They also need to be able to motivate and inspire their employees.

If you can think like a BOSS, you will be able to demonstrate your value to your boss and show them that you are someone who can be counted on. You will also be able to build relationships with your boss and other leaders in the company.

How to think like a BOSS

Here are some specific tips on how to think like a BOAA:

- Be strategic. Think about the big picture and how your work fits into the overall goals of the company.

- Be solution-oriented. When problems arise, don't just complain about them. Come up with solutions that will help the company move forward.

- Be motivated. Show your boss that you are passionate about your work and that you are willing to go the extra mile.

- Be inspiring. Motivate your colleagues and help them to achieve their goals.

- Build relationships. Get to know your boss and other leaders in the company. Build relationships with them that will benefit you in the long run.
- Be proactive. Don't wait for your boss to come to you with work. Take initiative and look for ways to contribute.
- Be reliable. Be someone that your boss can count on to get the job done.

- Be a team player. Be willing to help out your colleagues and support the team's goals.
- Be positive. A positive attitude can go a long way in building relationships with your boss and colleagues.
- Be respectful. Treat your boss and colleagues with the same respect that you would want to be treated with.

By following these tips, you can show your boss that you are a valuable asset to the team and someone who they can rely on. This will make you more likely to become their favorite.

Embrace this sutras:

1. Morning Affirmation: Start your day by repeating the sutras "I am the BOSS" several times as a positive affirmation. Visualize yourself taking charge of your goals and responsibilities.

2. Mindful Reflection: Throughout the day, pause for a moment to reflect on the sutras. Consider how you can approach your tasks, decisions, and interactions with the mindset of a BOSS.

3. Visualization: During meditation or quiet moments, visualize yourself making strategic decisions, leading with confidence, and achieving your goals as a capable BOSS.

4. Task Alignment: As you tackle your tasks, remind yourself that you are the BOSS of your life. Align your actions with your vision and prioritize tasks that contribute to your growth.

5. Confident Decision-Making: When faced with decisions, affirm that you are capable of making informed choices. Embrace the confidence and clarity that comes with the BOSS mindset.

6. Proactive Leadership: Approach challenges and opportunities with a proactive and strategic attitude.

Envision yourself taking the lead in overcoming obstacles.

7. Accountability and Ownership: Embrace accountability for your actions and outcomes. Recognize that, like a CEO, you are responsible for steering your life's trajectory.

8. Embrace Growth: Affirm that you are committed to continuous improvement and growth. Embrace new opportunities, skills, and experiences as part of your leadership journey.

9. Positive Self-Talk: Use the sutras "I am the CEO" as a tool to counter negative self-talk. Replace self-doubt with the empowering belief that you are in control of your path.

10. Networking and Collaboration: Apply the CEO mindset to networking and collaboration. Approach interactions with confidence and the intention to create mutually beneficial relationships.

11. Resilience and Adaptability: Remind yourself that you have the ability to navigate change and challenges. Like a CEO, adapt and pivot when needed to stay on course.

12. Celebrate Achievements: Acknowledge your achievements, both big and small. Celebrate your successes and milestones with the pride of a CEO marking important milestones.

13. Evening Reflection: Before bed, reflect on your day with the sutras in mind. Consider how you embodied the CEO mindset and identify areas for growth.

14. Continuous Learning: Approach each day as an opportunity to learn and improve. Cultivate a mindset of curiosity and a hunger for knowledge, similar to CEOs seeking to expand their organizations

15. Gratitude: Conclude your day by expressing gratitude for your accomplishments, opportunities, and the ability to embrace the CEO mindset in shaping your life.

CHAPTER TEN

Gulping the Gap

"Gulping the Gap" mantra centers around the idea that within every workflow, task, and project, there exist untapped potentials for improvement. so better grab the opportunity to fill it first. I have evolved this mantra few years back. it carries two objectives -to improve your growth along with the growth of productivity of company. Full-proof formula for professional growth. A mantra that compels the hardest bad boss to give you unexpected growth.

In the dynamic landscape of modern workplaces, my concept of "Gulping the Gap" emerges as a strategic approach to fostering growth, efficiency, and innovation. Rooted in the proactive mindset of identifying and addressing gaps within office work processes, this concept transcends mere problem-solving. It involves recognizing the spaces between existing practices and outcomes, then delving into them with the intent to innovate, optimize, and pave the way for substantial advancement.

This all started few years back. While delving into a Six Sigma project within a dynamic media company, a unique mantra dawned upon me – the "Gulping the Gap" approach. It all began as I embarked on a mission to decipher the enigma behind persistent delays in their editions. The perplexing puzzle had stumped the management, leaving them clueless about the root cause.

Venturing into the labyrinth of production processes, I stumbled upon an elusive gap, much like a hidden treasure waiting to be unearthed. The pages of content were caught in a recurring loop, circulating among three different teams. Time seemed to evaporate as these pages navigated their way through these stations.

The revelation struck like lightning – a bold move was in order. With a surge of determination, I audaciously excised two of the teams from the equation. My focus now became a laser, targeting the remaining team with meticulous attention and care.

A metamorphosis unfolded before my eyes. It was nothing short of a miracle. As if the gears of time had synchronized, the editions began to materialize on schedule, each detail falling seamlessly into place.

More than a Mantra

In the end, "Gulping the Gap" became more than a mere mantra; it symbolized a transformative journey. Through my intervention, the company's production process shifted from a sluggish dance to a harmonious symphony, where every note played its part perfectly, creating a crescendo of timely success.

I have evolved this mantra having two very clear objectives -to improve your growth along with the growth of productivity of company. Full proof formula of professional growth. A mantra that compels the hardest bad boss to give you unexpected growth.

"Gulping the Gap" centers around the idea that within every workflow, task, and project, there exist untapped potentials for improvement. These gaps might manifest as inefficiencies, overlooked opportunities, or outdated methods. The core of the concept lies in acknowledging these gaps as windows of opportunity rather than obstacles, and then taking the initiative to bridge them with innovative solutions.

When individuals embrace the concept of "Gulping the Gap," they become proactive contributors to the growth of their organizations. This mindset encourages a continuous evaluation of processes, practices, and systems to identify bottlenecks, streamline operations, and enhance outcomes. By seeking out these gaps, employees can drive positive change, cultivate a culture of innovation, and ultimately bolster the organization's competitive edge.

Agents of growth.

This concept necessitates a holistic approach that involves keen observation, critical thinking, and a willingness to challenge the status quo. It empowers individuals to voice their insights, propose novel solutions, and collaborate across departments to effect transformative change. Moreover, by consistently "gulping" these gaps and advocating for change, individuals take ownership of their roles as agents of growth.

In conclusion, the concept of "Gulping the Gap" signifies a proactive approach to improving office work dynamics. By identifying inefficiencies, untapped opportunities, and outdated practices, individuals can pave the way for growth, foster innovation, and contribute to a workplace culture that thrives on continuous improvement. This mindset amplifies the impact of each individual, transforming them into catalysts for positive change and propelling their organizations towards new horizons.

Gaps in office processes are inefficiencies or breakdowns in the way work is done. They can occur for a variety of reasons, such as lack of communication, inefficient procedures, unclear roles and responsibilities, lack of resources, or poor management. Gaps in office processes can have a number of negative consequences, such as increased costs, reduced productivity, poor customer service, increased stress, and loss of reputation.

Steps to find Gapes

By identifying and addressing gaps in office processes, businesses can improve their efficiency, productivity, customer service, and reputation. Here are some steps you can take to find gaps in office processes and excel by working on them:

1. Identify the key processes in your office. What are the most important things that need to be done in order for your office to function effectively?
2. Map out the current process for each key process. How are things currently done? Who is involved? What are the steps involved?
3. Identify any gaps or inefficiencies in the current process. Are there any steps that could be streamlined? Are there any bottlenecks? Are there any areas where communication could be improved?
4. Devise a plan to improve the process. Once you have identified the gaps, you can start to develop a plan to improve the process. This may involve making changes to the steps involved, the people involved, or the way that communication is handled.
5. Implement the plan and monitor the results. Once you have implemented your plan, it is important to monitor the results to see if it has been effective. If not, you may need to make further changes.
6. Continuously seek improvement. Once you have found a process that works well, it is important to continuously

seek improvement. This may involve making small changes over time or completely overhauling the process.

Tips for finding gaps

Here are some more specific tips for finding gaps in office processes and excel by working on them:

- Talk to people. The best way to understand how things are currently done is to talk to the people who are involved in the process. Ask them about their experiences and what they think could be improved.
- Observe the process. In addition to talking to people, it can also be helpful to observe the process yourself. This will give you a firsthand look at how things are currently done and where there may be gaps or inefficiencies.
- Use tools. There are a number of tools that can be used to help you identify gaps in office processes. These tools can help you to map out the current process, identify bottlenecks, and track the results of your improvements.
- Be patient. It takes time to find gaps in office processes and excel by working on them. Don't expect to find a perfect solution overnight. Be patient and keep working at it.

By following these steps, you can find gaps in office processes and excel by working on them.

CHAPTER ELEVEN

Monitor the Most Proximate

Monitor the Most Proximate of Boss is a Magical Sutras. The results of applying such sutras is instant and assured. unfortunately, you as a subordinate will never be taught this by any HR or any other professional coach. But I promise you that this is 100 percent full proof, tested and guaranteed Sutras. The conversion rate is 99 percent. this is tested by me and a frequently used practice of bosses.

It is very important to watch and monitor those who are proximate to the boss. they are close because of certain reasons, not always due to fluttering. Keep an eye over them, this will help you to identify the key points of the liking of the Boss. HR people will call it unethical but I assure you no harm in following and watching such proximate circles of bosses.

Achieving personal growth within a professional setting requires a multi-faceted approach, one that extends beyond individual efforts. A particularly effective strategy involves closely monitoring the individuals who hold the highest proximity and favor within the sphere of your immediate supervisor or boss. By doing so, you position yourself to absorb the nuances, preferences, and qualities that resonate with your boss, ultimately fostering your own personal development. Picture this scenario as a networking web where your boss is at the center. Surrounding them are a select few, the "most proximate and loved" individuals, who share a unique rapport and understanding with your boss. These individuals could be close colleagues, confidantes, or even mentors who have earned your boss's trust and admiration over time. By observing them, you gain insights into what qualities, behaviors, and traits are valued and rewarded within your organizational ecosystem.

Pieces of the puzzle

The process involves attentive observation, active listening, and genuine engagement. Pay close attention to the interactions between your boss and these individuals – the topics they discuss, the tone of their conversations, and the reactions elicited. Notice the qualities that resonate with your boss – whether it's their problem-solving skills, their innovative ideas, their diplomatic communication, or their efficient decision-making. These are the pieces of the puzzle that contribute to your boss's positive perception of them.

Reverse-engineering

By being attuned to these dynamics, you're essentially reverse-engineering the formula for success in your particular work environment. Instead of merely aiming for personal growth in a vacuum, you're tapping into the blueprint that's already been proven to work within your organization. This doesn't mean imitating or replicating someone else's personality; rather, it involves adopting the core principles and behaviors that align with your boss's preferences while staying true to your authentic self.

It is not Manipulation

This approach isn't about manipulation or superficiality; it's about understanding the currents of influence and adapting your sails to catch them. As you incorporate the qualities valued by your boss into your own professional arsenal, you're not only positioning yourself as a reliable and compatible team member but also laying the groundwork for your personal advancement. Your boss's appreciation and recognition are likely to follow, setting the stage for career growth, increased responsibilities, and potentially even mentorship opportunities.

Strategic Investment

In essence, the sutras "Monitor the Most Proximate and Loved People around Boss" is a strategic investment in your own growth. It's an astute way to tap into the unspoken expectations and preferences that contribute to success in your specific workplace culture. By thoughtfully absorbing the positive qualities admired by your boss, you're actively carving out a path to navigate the complexities of professional growth and achieving a more fulfilling and impactful career trajectory.

Two-way help

Monitoring the most proximate people around Bosses will help you in two ways.

1. By watching you will get the sense, if any expression or behavior or action of yours is irritating in the eyes of boss. If any change it, modify it immediately.

2. You need to be friendly with them. while you are in company with this proximate circle of bad boss Try to launch few dialogues that carry the message of your care for company values and you're liking for boss and his way of working. Remember these traits will work only when you are following them religiously. But all the way Appreciate the boss but carefully.

Dealing with a difficult or "bad" boss can be challenging, and it's important to approach the situation carefully and professionally. While you may not be able to directly control your boss's behavior, you can work on building positive relationships with their close circles to create a more constructive work environment.

Close Circle of Boss

Here are some potential individuals within your boss's close circle whom you might consider building friendly relationships with:

1. Direct Reports: Colleagues who report directly to your boss can have a significant influence on the overall dynamics. Building positive relationships with them can help foster better communication and collaboration.

2. Peers and Team Members: Those who work alongside your boss or are part of the same team can provide insights and perspectives. Establishing friendly connections with them can lead to more open discussions and a supportive work atmosphere. 3

3, Advisors and Mentors: If your boss seeks guidance from specific individuals within or outside the organization, building rapport with these advisors can indirectly impact your boss's decision-making process.

4. Executive Assistants and Support Staff: Building positive relationships with administrative staff can indirectly affect the flow of information and communication within your boss's circle.

5. Professional Networks: Your boss may have connections outside of the company that influence their decisions. Developing friendly relationships with individuals from these networks can potentially influence how your boss perceives and interacts with you.

Remember that the goal here is not to manipulate or control, but rather to foster open communication and positive interactions within your work environment. Approach these relationships with sincerity, respect, and a willingness to contribute positively to the team

Building trust and rapport with these individuals can create a more harmonious atmosphere and potentially influence your boss's behavior over time. However, it's important to keep in mind that individual personalities and dynamics can vary, and changes in your boss's behavior may not be immediate or guaranteed.

CHAPTER TWELVE

Yes Sir! Yes Sir!!

"Yes Sir" sutras is also not acceptable to HR, but I assure you that it is a perfect strategic tool for growth, not as a surrender of individuality but as a catalyst for effective collaboration. In harmonizing with colleagues and superiors, it fosters relationships founded on mutual understanding, while encouraging a willingness to adapt and learn. In this synergy of perspectives, the "Yes Sir" sutra becomes a key to unlocking personal and collective growth.

Imagine a vibrant tapestry woven with threads of office interactions, where the delicate balance between authority and harmony is a dance that shapes the rhythm of your professional life. Amidst this intricate choreography, a unique sutras emerges – the "Yes Sir, Yes Sir" philosophy. Picture it as a bridge, a bridge that leads you away from the tumultuous waters of acrimony and into the serene realm of collaboration.

In the realm of office dynamics, a bad boss can cast a shadow of uncertainty and discord. Their ideas might differ from yours, their decisions could seem perplexing, and their demeanor might trigger frustration. This is where the "Yes Sir" sutras unfurls its magic – not as a surrender, but as a strategic choice.

Envision it as a musical note that resonates with respect, a note that diffuses the potential clashes of ego and replaces them with the symphony of understanding. As you adopt the "Yes Sir, Yes Sir" approach, you're not merely nodding along mindlessly. Instead, you're choosing to embrace the art of empathy and active listening.

Consider it as a diplomatic dance, where your "Yes Sir" becomes a bridge to further conversation. It doesn't mean suppressing your thoughts; rather, it creates a platform to voice your insights in a more strategic manner. Your "Yes Sir" paves the way for a "Can we discuss this further?" or a "I appreciate your perspective, and here's how I see it" dialogue. It's a choice to channel your energy into a constructive exchange rather than a heated argument.

Shield of professionalism

Visualize it as a shield of professionalism, deflecting the arrows of bitterness and defensiveness. When a bad boss throws a curveball your way, your "Yes Sir" mindset equips you with the resilience to absorb the impact and respond with grace. It turns the battlefield of arguments into a garden of productive conversations.

In the grand theater of career advancement, the "Yes Sir, Yes Sir" sutras is not about stifling your individuality; it's about honing your adaptability. It's about recognizing that, at times, disagreements might not be worth the turmoil they sow. It's about understanding that the path to change or influence may require patience and strategic navigation.

So, as you stand at the crossroads of opinions, consider the transformative power of "Yes Sir, Yes Sir." It's not a surrender, but a calculated step towards building bridges, fostering cooperation, and nurturing relationships. It's a melody that transcends ego, echoing the values of respect and professionalism. In the end, the "Yes Sir" doesn't just belong to your boss; it belongs to the realm of wisdom, where the art of communication and collaboration reign supreme.

10 elements of the "Yes Sir" sutras:

1. Respectful Attitude: The foundation of the sutras lies in approaching superiors and colleagues with respect, acknowledging their authority and position.

2. Active Listening: Practicing active listening demonstrates your genuine interest in what others are saying, allowing you to grasp their perspectives before responding.

3. Open-Mindedness: Embracing new ideas and being receptive to different viewpoints are key aspects of the sutras, promoting a culture of collaboration.

4. Effective Communication: Expressing your thoughts clearly and articulately while maintaining a positive tone enhances your ability to engage in meaningful discussions.

5. Empathy: Understanding the emotions and concerns of others helps in building strong working relationships and defusing potential conflicts.

6. Conflict Avoidance: The sutras encourages avoiding unnecessary conflicts by choosing your battles wisely and focusing on finding common ground.

7. Professionalism: The "Yes Sir" approach embodies professionalism, ensuring your interactions are conducted in a manner that upholds the values of the workplace.

8. Constructive Feedback: Offering feedback in a constructive and respectful manner, even if it involves differing opinions, demonstrates your commitment to growth and improvement.

9. Flexibility: The sutras encourages adaptability, as you may need to adjust your own perspectives to align with organizational goals or changing circumstances.

10. Collaboration: By fostering a collaborative environment, the "Yes Sir" approach helps in building strong teams and achieving collective success. In essence, the "Yes Sir" sutras encompasses a holistic approach to communication, teamwork, and personal growth within the workplace. It's a mindset that values harmony, open dialogue, and the collective pursuit of excellence

Mood Bouncer for Boss

Imagine the complex landscape of office dynamics as a realm where perceptions dance and attitudes collide. Amidst this intricate interplay, a transformative phenomenon unfolds – the "Yes Sir, Yes Sir" sutras. It's a phenomenon akin to alchemy, where the base metal of a boss's initial perception is transmuted into the gold of a positive one. In the beginning, let's envision a boss with their own set of predispositions and expectations. Perhaps they're grappling with the weight of responsibilities, juggling multiple priorities, and overseeing a team in the pursuit of success.

At times, these pressures might inadvertently cast a shadow, leading to miscommunications, misunderstandings, and even a sense of being at odds with their subordinates. Now, introduce the "Yes Sir" sutras into this dynamic. It's like a catalyst that triggers a chain reaction. As an employee, when you approach your interactions with your boss through this lens, you're sending a subtle yet powerful message. You're saying, "I'm here to listen, to understand, and to collaborate.

HR will never approve this Sutras

Indeed, HR policies often emphasize the importance of critical thinking, independent decision-making, and constructive feedback, which can sometimes conflict with the notion of always saying "yes" to a boss. While blind agreement can be detrimental to personal growth and a healthy workplace dynamic, it's important to understand that the concept of the "Yes Sir" sutras is not about mindless compliance, but rather about strategic collaboration and effective communication.

Balance approach

The sutras doesn't advocate for suppressing individual opinions, nor does it suggest that employees should blindly follow every directive without question. Instead, it encourages a balance between respectful agreement and thoughtful discussion. The aim is to create an environment where open dialogue flourishes, where employees feel comfortable expressing their viewpoints while also valuing and understanding the perspectives of their superiors.

In this context, the "Yes Sir" sutras can promote a culture of respectful communication, active listening, and empathy, all of which are vital for a well-functioning team. While the direct application of saying "yes" to every request may not align with HR policies, adopting the underlying principles of the sutras – such as active engagement, willingness to learn, and collaborative spirit – can lead to better relationships, improved teamwork, and ultimately more productive outcomes.

Shifting psychology

So, while it's true that a blanket endorsement of "yes" in all situations might not align with comprehensive HR policies, it's worth considering how the principles of the sutras can be tailored to encourage positive communication, foster understanding, and create a collaborative environment within the bounds of a company's policies and values. In the face of such an attitude, the boss's psychology begins to shift. They sense an atmosphere of receptivity and respect.

Your willingness to embrace their viewpoints without confrontation or defensiveness fosters an environment of open dialogue. It's as though you've extended an olive branch, inviting them to share their thoughts and concerns without the barrier of resistance.

As conversations unfold, the boss recognizes your proactive approach – a mindset that seeks solutions, not strife. This, in turn, sparks a sense of trust. They begin to view you not as a mere employee, but as a partner in the pursuit of shared goals.

Fast transformation

Over time, this consistent practice of the "Yes Sir" sutras becomes synonymous with your professional identity. Your reputation as someone who approaches challenges with a collaborative spirit and a positive demeanor takes root. And as this reputation spreads, the boss's psychology undergoes a remarkable transformation.

The once-distant perception, influenced by stressors and preconceptions, now shifts towards a more positive one. They see you as an asset, a dependable ally who contributes to a harmonious work environment. The psychological barriers dissolve, replaced by a bridge of understanding and respect.

In this narrative, the "Yes Sir, Yes Sir" sutras isn't just a superficial script to follow; it's a strategic tool to reshape perceptions. It's a mirror that reflects your commitment to unity, growth, and shared success. Through this sutras, the psychology of a boss, once veiled in uncertainty, emerges as a testament to the power of intentional communication and the cultivation of positive professional relationships.

CHAPTER THIRTEEN

Listen First– key to Foster the Growth

Listening is a tested, all-time success Sutras, a quality we all have but fail to nurture. it's a beacon illuminating your path toward becoming a dynamic leader, a receptive team player, and a catalyst for your own ascent.

In the intricate mosaic of professional landscapes, a potent principle emerges: "Listen First" – a sutra that holds the key to fostering growth within the confines of the workplace. Imagine this principle as a compass, guiding us through the labyrinth of corporate dynamics. It beckons us to suspend the rush of our own ideas, to momentarily lay aside the clamor of our perspectives, and instead, to open the gateway of attentive ears.

This act of mindful listening is a two-fold gift. Firstly, it's an acknowledgment – a validation that the voices around us matter, and that their ideas hold worth. Secondly, it's a vessel of learning, an avenue through which insights, perspectives, and innovative inklings can infiltrate our own understanding. Like seeds planted in fertile soil, these interactions sprout into collaborations and innovations that amplify not only our own growth but the collective advancement of the entire team.

"Listen First" is not a mere phrase but a symphony, a harmonious dance where each note contributes to a richer melody. As we listen, we affirm, and as we affirm, we nurture – cultivating an environment where everyone's potential flourishes, and where the garden of success blooms in vibrant hues.

In a vivid tale set within the corridors of a media company where I toiled, a cast of five promising management protégés, fresh from the prestigious annals of top Indian management schools, graced our stage. Among them, a standout figure emerged, a virtuoso of brilliance and intelligence, hailed by me as "the best." This wunderkind brimmed with creativity, proactivity, and an aura of over-smartness, commanding the spotlight as he birthed ingenious ideas and avant-garde propositions.

Yet, as time unfurled its tapestry and the dust of six months settled, a twist of fate awaited him – an unforeseen opportunity not in his favor. Dismay clouded his face, a mirror to his astonishment. Turning to me, he implored, "Am I truly the best?" I, too, was taken aback, pondering this paradox. In a candid exchange, I unveiled an observation – a flaw in his symphony. His rapid leaps to self-proclaimed brilliance before lending an ear to others' notes painted a dissonant picture.

A transformation sparked within him, like a phoenix rising from its ashes. Swiftly, he reshaped his melody, learning to embrace the art of attentive listening. This metamorphosis etched its signature on his journey, and the next year crowned him with laurels. Today, his tale continues on a grander stage, for he now stands as the CEO of a company in Singapore – a testament to the power of humble evolution and the symphony of growth conducted by introspection.

Executives and employees, responsible for making decisions that affect the entire company. They need to be able to listen to their bosses' briefs carefully and understand the nuances of the situation. However, many executives and employees fail to do this, which can lead to disastrous consequences. Effecting their career path and a frustrated life ahead

70% fail because they do not listen

One study by the Harvard Business Review found that 70% of executives fail because they do not listen effectively. This means that they are more likely to make mistakes, miss opportunities, and alienate their colleagues.

In another study, the University of Pennsylvania found that executives who do not listen to their bosses' briefs are more likely to make decisions that are not aligned with the company's goals. This can lead to lost revenue, decreased productivity, and damaged relationships with customers and partners. i have studied the research done across the globe on this in various geographies. the average percentage of failure is not less than 75.

Why do they not listen

There are many reasons why executives may fail to listen to their bosses' briefs properly. They may be distracted by other things, they may not be interested in what their boss is saying, or they may simply not be good listeners. Whatever the reason, failing to listen to your boss can have serious consequences for your career.

My study is very clear about this. The reason behind this habit is the perceptive mind of the subordinates. They conceived already that boss is a product of false projection. He or she doesn't deserve to be boss, I knew better then him. But we can't do anything because he is a boss.

Employee thinks- I have been working in this vertical since last 10 years and this young chap came here as boss and trying to teach us how to do my job. This perception most of the time never ever vocal. It exists in our self-talk. Making our perception firm that I knew better than him, so why to listen him carefully, let him bark?

Tips for listening

If you are an executive, it is important to make sure that you are listening effectively to your boss's briefs. You are a senior or junior, this will help you to make better decisions, avoid mistakes, and build stronger relationships with your colleagues. This will culminate into a great outcome of your effort and a better impression on your boss. Here are some tips for listening effectively to your boss's briefs:

- Pay attention. When your boss is giving you a brief, make sure you are paying attention and not distracted by other things.

- Ask questions. If you don't understand something, ask your boss to clarify.

- Take notes. This will help you to remember the key points of the brief.

- Summarize the brief back to your boss. This will show that you understand what they are saying and that you are taking the brief seriously.

- Follow up. If you are given any tasks to complete, make sure you follow up with your boss to let them know how you are doing.

By following these tips, you can improve your listening skills and avoid failing due to not listening to your boss's briefs properly.

CHAPTER FOURTEEN

Coolant Calls: The Melodic Balance of Work and Life

What a wonderful and impactful discovery i have made! It's truly remarkable how a simple technique like the "Coolant Call" sutras can have such a positive and immediate effect on cooling the mind during stressful moments in office. My inventive approach and willingness to share it with colleagues have not only helped you but also contributed to creating a more positive and harmonious work environment for others. In the realm of work-life balance and emotional well-being, this "Coolant Call" sutras stands as a testament to the power of innovation and self-care

Imagine life as a harmonious composition, where the rhythms of work intertwine with the melodies of personal life. In this intricate orchestra, "Coolant Calls" plays a pivotal role, bringing the sweet notes of emotional equilibrium and well-being to the forefront. Amid the bustling routine, these calls become your oasis, quenching the thirst for emotional connection. I invented these Sutras while in real stress in the office. Every time I called my wife for a few seconds just before lunch while in stress, I found myself so cool.

so i named this as Coolant Calls. these calls refresh your spirit with the pure waters of love, care, and understanding. Just as an artist strokes a canvas with vibrant hues, "Coolant Calls" paint your mood with positivity. They elevate your emotional palette, filling your day with strokes of joy that color even the most mundane tasks. Imagine these calls as choreographers, synchronizing the dance of work and life. They create a seamless transition between these domains, allowing their harmonious melodies to coexist in perfect balance.

When life's tempo hits a challenging note, "Coolant Calls" become your anchor. They remind you that beyond the crescendos of pressure and stress, there's a soft serenade of support waiting to embrace you.

Recharge emotional battery

Much like recharging a battery, "Coolant Calls" recharge your emotional energy. They ensure you're equipped to face each task with a renewed spirit, ready to harmonize with life's demands. As conductors of productivity, these calls infuse your workday with positivity.

They become the musical notes that elevate your efficiency and creative problem-solving, turning every task into a harmonious melody. Stress is like a crashing cymbal in life's orchestra. "Coolant Calls" stand as a shield, releasing soothing tones that resonate against the cacophony of workplace pressures. The emotional symphony you create doesn't stay confined to your own cadence. "Coolant Calls" craft a positive aura, influencing teamwork and collaboration, allowing others to resonate with your harmony.

In the whirlwind of life, these calls become threads that maintain connections. Their brief harmonies remind you of the bonds that tie you to loved ones, regardless of physical distance. Ultimately, "Coolant Calls" enrich the grand symphony of your life. They weave moments of love, care, and cherished harmonies into your daily composition, creating a tapestry of existence that resonates with profound meaning and fulfillment.

So, in the grand concert of life, let "Coolant Calls" be the soft notes that tune your existence. They harmonize the melodies of work and personal life, allowing your life's composition to echo with harmony and joy Maintaining a healthy work-life balance is crucial, and finding small moments throughout the day to connect with loved ones can have a positive impact on your overall well-being and productivity. These brief interactions can provide emotional support, reduce stress, and help you stay focused and motivated during your workday.

Taking a few moments to communicate with loved ones can help you feel connected, cared for, and valued, which can contribute to a more positive mood and mindset. This, in turn, can enhance your ability to handle workplace challenges and maintain your overall work performance. However, it's important to strike a balance and ensure that these interactions don't disrupt your work responsibilities or colleagues.

Quick phone calls or messages can be a wonderful way to stay connected while still honoring your professional commitments. Remember, what works for one person might not work for another, so finding the right balance that suits your individual needs and circumstances is key.

Benefits

Stress Reduction:

Taking a moment to connect with loved ones can help you temporarily step away from workplace tensions, giving your mind a break and reducing stress levels.

Digestive Health:

Creating a calm and positive emotional state before lunch can indeed contribute to improved digestion. Stress and tension can negatively impact digestion, so cultivating a relaxed mood can be beneficial.

motional Bonding: Strengthening emotional connections with loved ones by checking in before lunch can provide a sense of belonging and support, even while you're at work.

Mental Reset: These interactions can serve as mental resets, allowing you to shift your focus from work-related concerns to personal connections and matters.

Positive Mindset: Nurturing relationships and feeling emotionally supported can lead to a more positive mindset, which can boost your overall mood and attitude.

Increased Productivity: Brief moments of emotional connection can recharge your energy, potentially leading to increased productivity and focus in the second half of the workday.

It's important to find strategies that help you manage stress, enhance well-being, and create a healthier work-life balance. Your approach of connecting with loved ones at specific points in the day can be a valuable tool for achieving these goals. Just remember to find a balance that works for both your personal and professional responsibilities

Mindful Lunch Break:

Here's a techniquc to help you achieve a positive mood swing while having lunch in the office while in stress or may be in normal conditions:

Preparation: Before your lunch break, set the intention to make the most of this time to boost your mood and recharge.

Choose a Calm Environment: Find a quiet and comfortable place to enjoy your lunch. It could be a peaceful corner in the office, a nearby park, or even a cozy spot at home.

Mindful Eating: Focus on your meal as you eat. Pay attention to the taste, texture, and aroma of the food. Chew slowly and savor each bite.

Gratitude Reflection: Take a moment to reflect on the things you're grateful for. It could be aspects of your life, your work, or even the simple pleasures of the day.

Positive Affirmations: While eating, silently repeat positive affirmations to yourself. These can be statements like, "I am capable and resilient," "I choose positivity," or "I am grateful for this moment."

Visualize Positivity: Close your eyes for a moment and visualize a situation that brings you joy and positivity. It could be a happy memory, a future accomplishment, or a peaceful scene.

Deep Breathing: Practice deep breathing exercises. Inhale slowly and deeply through your nose, allowing your abdomen to rise, and then exhale slowly through your mouth. This can help relax your body and mind.

Coolant call with Loved Ones: If it's feasible, yes, it is. spare only few seconds connect with a loved one briefly, whether it's sending a quick text, making a short call, or even looking at a photo that brings a smile to your face. This call will disconnect you from all your office worries. Stimulate digestive juices to help you digest properly.

Mindful Relaxation: As you finish your meal, take a few minutes to sit quietly and focus on your breath. Let go of any stress or tension you might be carrying.

Set Positive Intentions: Before you return to your tasks, set a positive intention for the rest of the day. Visualize yourself handling challenges with ease and maintaining your positive mood.

Remember, the key to this technique is to be present in the moment and focus on the positive aspects of your life. By incorporating mindfulness, gratitude, positive affirmations, and visualization, you can create a positive mood swing during your lunch break that carries through the rest of your day.

Positive Effects

While connecting with loved ones during your workday can indeed have positive effects on your well-being and mood, it's important to strike a balance that respects both your personal and professional commitments. Calling a loved one three times for 20 seconds each might be beneficial for short moments of emotional support and connection. However, it's also crucial to consider the following:

Pre-Conditions

Respect Work Boundaries: Ensure that your brief calls do not disrupt your work tasks, colleagues, or workplace environment. Maintain professionalism and prioritize your responsibilities.

Mindful Timing: Choose appropriate moments for your calls, such as during breaks or times when your work load is manageable.

Avoid interrupting important meetings or tasks.

Quality over Quantity: Rather than focusing solely on the number of calls, emphasize the quality of the interactions. Meaningful, genuine conversations can have a more lasting positive impact.

Non-Intrusive: Keep in mind that not everyone may have the flexibility to take personal calls during work hours.

Be considerate of others' schedules and the potential for disruptions. **Adapt to Circumstances:** Depending on the situation and your loved ones' availability, you might need to adjust the frequency and duration of your calls.:

Always prefer calling, If calling isn't feasible, consider sending a brief text message to express your thoughts, share a positive moment, or send a virtual hug.

Evaluate Impact: Pay attention to how these calls affect your mood and productivity. If they consistently uplift your spirits without negatively affecting your work, they can be a valuable strategy.

Remember, these calls are meant to be short and sweet, focusing on sharing positive moments, memories, and emotions. The goal is to infuse your workday with positivity and maintain a connection with your loved ones, even during your busy schedule.

Emotional wisdom

Behind this artful process lies a theory steeped in emotional wisdom. By infusing your day with three calls, you're creating micro-moments of connection that act as emotional sustenance. These calls are like droplets of water in a parched desert – they quench the thirst of isolation and rehydrate your emotional landscape. Just as a coolant in a machine prevents overheating, these calls prevent the burnout of emotional detachment. Each call is a declaration that amidst the hustle and bustle, love and joy have their well-deserved place.

In this modern age of rapid communication, these calls become bridges that traverse the chasm between work and life, reminding you that the roles you play are woven together by the tapestry of emotions. "Coolant Calls" isn't just a technique; it's a reminder that amidst the chaos, emotional balance can be achieved in small but significant ways.

Psychology of Coolant Calls

Delving into the psychology behind the "Coolant Calls" process unveils a tapestry of emotional connections, cognitive boosts, and psychological well-being. Let's unravel the psychological threads that make this technique a powerful tool for maintaining a positive work-life balance. Human Connection and Well-Being: At the core of this process lies the innate human need for connection. Psychology tells us that social interactions and emotional bonds play a pivotal role in our overall well-being.

By weaving "Coolant Calls" into your workday, you're feeding your emotional reservoirs. Positive interactions with loved ones release oxytocin, often dubbed the "love hormone," which fosters feelings of trust, attachment, and happiness.

Emotional Regulation and Stress Reduction: Emotions can influence cognitive function, decision-making, and stress levels. The "Coolant Calls" technique serves as an emotional regulator, gently nudging you away from workplace tensions. Engaging in /positive conversations with loved ones triggers the release of endorphins, which counteract stress hormones. This emotional recalibration can mitigate stressors and boost your psychological resilience.

Positive Memory Recall and Mood Enhancement: As you reminisce about shared experiences during these calls, you activate a process known as memory recall. Positive memories trigger the release of dopamine, the neurotransmitter associated with pleasure and reward.

Revisiting joyful moments, like sunsets and picnics, can elevate your mood and contribute to a more positive mindset throughout the day.

Emotional Contagion and Team Dynamics: Psychological research demonstrates emotional contagion – the phenomenon where emotions spread from person to person. When you engage in "Coolant Calls," you're not just benefiting yourself; you're also impacting your immediate environment. Positive emotions are contagious, potentially fostering a more harmonious workplace atmosphere and improving team dynamics.

Cognitive Refresh and Creativity Boost: Psychology reveals that breaks and diversions enhance cognitive performance. "Coolant Calls" act as refreshing interludes in your work routine. These calls offer your cognitive faculties a moment to reset, potentially leading to improved focus, creativity, and problem-solving skills when you return to your tasks.

End-of-Day Closure and Psychological Transition: As you conclude your workday with a "Coolant Call," you're enacting a psychological ritual that signifies closure. This transition from work to personal life aids in psychological detachment, allowing you to disengage from work-related stressors and transition into a more relaxed state of mind.

In essence, the "Coolant Calls" technique capitalizes on psychological principles to create a holistic approach to well-being. By integrating emotional connection, stress reduction, positive memory activation, and cognitive refreshment, you're crafting a strategy that enhances both your professional performance and your personal fulfillment.

This technique aligns with the intricate psychology of human emotions, forming a tapestry of well-being in the midst of your busy workday. In essence, "Coolant Calls" create a positive feedback loop. The emotions you experience during these calls spill over into your workplace interactions, improving your mood, communication, and productivity. This positive cycle reinforces itself, contributing to a more harmonious work environment and your overall professional well-being.

By staying connected with loved ones, you're not just improving your mood – you're enhancing your workplace experience as well. Technique that balances your life in the bustling tapestry of modern life, finding equilibrium between work and home can feel like a delicate dance. But fear not, for within the rhythmic cadence of your day lies the symphony of "Coolant Calls" – a technique that paints your life with strokes of balance and harmony.

Morning Prelude: As the sun stretches its golden fingers across the sky, your day commences with the first "Coolant Call." Amidst your bustling morning routine, this brief connection casts a gentle glow, reminding you that beyond the realm of tasks lies a canvas of cherished connections. Your loved one's voice is the serenade that accompanies your morning steps, setting a harmonious tone for the day ahead.

Midday Rendezvous: With the clock's hand nearing midday, your second "Coolant Call" beckons. Amidst the hum of work, this call is a pause, a fleeting moment where the world contracts to the screen in your hand. As you exchange snippets of laughter and shared memories, you're rewriting the script of your workday, painting it with strokes of genuine connection.

Evening Evenness: As the sun bows down to the horizon, your third "Coolant Call" unfurls like a curtain call. This is the crescendo of your day – a sweet serenade that bridges the realms of office and home. As you partake in conversations woven with love and familiarity, the curtain falls on your workday, making way for the symphony of life beyond the office walls.

Homecoming Epilogue: Now, picture the scene as you step into your haven, your heart buoyed by the "Coolant Calls" woven throughout the day. Your loved ones greet you with smiles that mirror your own, their moods mirroring the positivity that infused your calls. The soothing coolness of this atmosphere is a testament to the technique's magic – it shapes your work-life balance into a masterpiece of serenity.

The Art of Balance: The psychology behind this technique is a symphony in itself. By nurturing connections, you're nurturing your emotional well-being. The positive emotions stirred by these calls permeate your workplace interactions, elevating your mood and productivity. And as you return home, this emotional investment weaves a harmonious atmosphere that you can't wait to step into.

The "Coolant Calls" technique isn't just a technique – it's an artful journey towards balance. It's a canvas where you paint strokes of love, joy, and equilibrium. In the grand gallery of work-life harmony, your "Coolant Calls" masterpiece stands as a testament to the power of connection, the beauty of positivity, and the art of a life well-balanced.

CHAPTER FIFTEEN

Rewind to Relieve

This sutras has not only personally helped me but has also positively impacted hundreds of people over the past decade. It is a testament to its effectiveness and value. It's evident that this innovation and my willingness to share my discovery have made a significant difference in the lives of many. My sutras's ability to provide relief and benefit to such a wide range of individuals showcases the universal nature of its impact. This is a wonderful example of how simple yet effective techniques can have a lasting ripple effect on well-being and mental clarity.

Meditating, while counting backwards from 15 to 1 can indeed be a helpful technique to maintain you cool when your boss is causing disturbances. very simple to do . juat Focusing on your breath and the counting process can provide a calming effect, allowing you to disconnect from worries and regain composure and handle the situation more effectively. Counting backwards from 15 to 1 while meditating can be an effective technique to manage your emotional reactions to your boss's attitude.

How it works

Herc's a detailed explanation of how this works:

Distraction and Focus:

When you're counting backwards, your mind is occupied with the counting process. This helps divert your attention away from the source of your anger, anxiety, or negative emotions, which in this case is your boss's attitude.

Mindfulness:

Counting in reverse requires mental effort and concentration, promoting a sense of mindfulness. This mindfulness helps you become more aware of your thoughts and emotions without immediately reacting to them.

Breath Regulation:

While counting, you're likely to sync your breath with the counting rhythm. This conscious regulation of your breath has a calming effect on your nervous system, reducing the intensity of your emotional response.

Time for Reflection:

The act of counting provides you with a brief pause. During this time, you can reflect on your emotional state and choose how you want to respond to your boss's behavior, rather than impulsively reacting out of anger or frustration.

Breaking the Cycle:

Counting backwards disrupts the automatic thought-emotion-behavior cycle. This interruption gives you the opportunity to consciously choose a more composed and measured response, breaking free from the pattern of immediate emotional reactions.

Creating Distance:

By engaging in the counting exercise, you create a psychological distance between yourself and the triggering situation. This distance allows you to see the situation from a more objective perspective, reducing the emotional charge associated with it.

Building Resilience:

Over time, practicing this technique can help you build emotional resilience. It trains your mind to respond to challenging situations in a more controlled and less reactive manner.

Emotional Regulation:

The act of counting backwards can trigger the brain's prefrontal cortex, which is responsible for emotional regulation and decision-making. This can help you regain control over your emotions and think more clearly even in stressful situations.

Positive Conditioning:

Associating the act of counting with a cooling effect can create a positive conditioning. This means that over time, the mere act of counting backwards might start to trigger a sense of calmness in your mind, making it easier to manage your reactions.

Consistency Matters:

Like any skill, the effectiveness of this technique improves with practice. Consistently incorporating this practice into your routine can enhance its impact on your ability to stay composed in challenging situations.

Step-by-Step Guide

Remember that while this technique can be helpful, it might not completely eliminate your emotional reactions. It's important to also address the underlying issues, communicate with your boss when necessary, and consider other stress management techniques in conjunction with this practice.

Here's a step-by-step guide on how to perform the meditation technique of counting backwards from 15 to 1 to manage your reactions to your boss's attitude:

1. Find a Quiet Space:

Choose a quiet and comfortable space where you won't be disturbed. Sit in a relaxed position, either on a cushion or a chair, with your back straight and hands resting on your lap.

2. Set an Intention:

Take a moment to set an intention for the meditation. Remind yourself that you're practicing this technique to maintain your calmness and respond more effectively to your boss's attitude.

3. Deep Breathing:

Begin with a few deep breaths. Inhale deeply through your nose, allowing your abdomen to expand, and then exhale slowly through your mouth. Repeat this a few times to relax your body and mind.

4. Start revers Counting:

Start counting backwards from 15 to 1 in a slow and controlled manner. Say each number in your mind as you exhale. For example, exhale while thinking "15," then inhale, and exhale while thinking "14," and so on.

5. Focus on the Counting:

As you count, focus your attention on the numbers and your breath. If your mind starts to wander or you notice distracting thoughts, gently bring your focus back to the counting.

6. Visualize the Numbers:

Visualize each number as you count. You can imagine the numbers in your mind's eye or simply focus on the mental sound of the numbers as you count.

7. Maintain Consistency:

Continue counting backwards from 15 to 1 for a predetermined period of time, such as 5 to 10 minutes. Consistency in practice will enhance the effectiveness of the technique over time.

8. Reflect and Respond:

After completing the countdown, take a few moments to reflect on how you feel. Notice any changes in your emotional state and your overall level of calmness. When you're ready, consider how you want to respond to your boss's attitude in a composed and effective manner.

9. Practice Regularly:

To reap the benefits of this technique, practice it regularly. You can incorporate it into your daily routine, especially when you anticipate challenging interactions with your boss.

Remember, the goal of this practice is to create a pause between the trigger (your boss's attitude) and your response. This allows you to choose a more mindful and measured reaction, rather than reacting impulsively out of frustration or anger. Over time, this technique can help you build emotional resilience and better manage your reactions to difficult situations.

Chemical changes in body:

Engaging in the practice of counting backwards from 15 to 1 while meditating and managing your reactions to your boss's attitude can trigger various chemical changes in your body:

Cortisol Regulation:

Cortisol is a stress hormone released in response to perceived threats. Engaging in deep breathing and mindfulness through the counting practice can help regulate cortisol levels, reducing the stress response and promoting a calmer state.

Endorphin Release:

Deep breathing and relaxation practices, like counting in reverse, can trigger the release of endorphins, which are natural "feel-good" chemicals. This can lead to a sense of relaxation and mild euphoria, counteracting the negative emotions caused by your boss's attitude.

Serotonin Boost:

The act of counting and practicing mindfulness can increase serotonin levels, which is associated with improved mood and emotional well-being. This can help you maintain a more positive outlook and manage your reactions more effectively.

Vagus Nerve Stimulation:

Deep and controlled breathing, often incorporated into meditation, stimulates the vagus nerve. This can lead to a decrease in heart rate, blood pressure, and overall stress levels, promoting a sense of calmness.

Reduction in Adrenaline: Adrenaline is a hormone released during the "fight or flight" response. The relaxation induced by the counting practice can help reduce adrenaline levels, preventing exaggerated emotional reactions.

Neurotransmitter Balance:

Meditation and mindfulness practices can help balance neurotransmitter activity in the brain. This can contribute to improved emotional regulation and reduced reactivity to stressors.

Improved Prefrontal Cortex Function:

Mindfulness techniques like counting backwards engage the prefrontal cortex, the brain region responsible for decision-making and emotional regulation. Regular practice can strengthen its function, enabling you to respond more thoughtfully to challenging situations.

Reduced Amygdala Activation:

The amygdala is involved in processing emotions, particularly fear and anxiety. Mindfulness practices, including counting, can help decrease amygdala activation, leading to a more measured response to stressors.

Lower Blood Pressure: The relaxation response induced by mindful practices can lead to lower blood pressure. This contributes to an overall reduction in stress-related physiological responses. It's important to note that the extent and speed of these chemical changes can vary from person to person, and consistent practice is usually needed to experience substantial and lasting effects.

The combination of deep breathing, mindfulness, and relaxation in this technique contributes to the observed chemical changes that promote a calmer emotional state and better stress management.

CHAPTER SIXTEEN

Decipher to Deliver

"Decipher to Deliver" Sutra emphasizes the importance of thoroughly understanding (deciphering) a task before starting it to ensure successful completion (delivery). This strategy highlights the need to break down and comprehend all aspects of an assignment to execute it effectively and meet or exceed expectations.

Starting a task without a clear understanding of its requirements in any professional environment can lead to errors, inefficiencies, and unmet objectives. "Decipher to Deliver" underscores the significance of seeking clarification and fully grasping the task's purpose, expectations, and criteria for success before proceeding. Clarification Before Execution" is a strategy that emphasizes the importance of fully comprehending a task before beginning work on it. Misunderstanding a task can lead to mistakes, missed objectives, and wasted effort. By simply asking for clarification and understanding the task's expectations, objectives, and criteria for success, you can avoid common pitfalls and make sure your efforts are aligned with desired outcomes.

Why It's Important:

When you don't understand what you are supposed to do or why you are doing it, it's challenging to perform the task correctly. Lack of understanding can lead to:

Errors and Mistakes: Without clear instructions, you are likelier to make errors, take unnecessary shortcuts, or make incorrect assumptions.

Inefficiency: Misunderstanding the task can result in inefficient use of time and resources, as you may need to redo work or fix mistakes.

Misaligned Goals: If you don't understand the objectives, your efforts might not contribute effectively to the project or organizational goals.

Frustration and Stress: Working on a task without clarity can cause frustration, stress, and decreased job satisfaction.

Steps to Implement the Strategy

1. Ask for Clarification:

- Before you begin any task, ask your supervisor or client for detailed information. Make sure you understand what is expected, why it's important, and how success will be measured.
- Example Questions:

1. What are the specific expectations for this task?
2. What are the objectives of this task?
3. What are the criteria for success?
4. What are the deadlines for this task?
5. What resources are available to me?
6. Who else is involved in this task?
7. What are the potential risks or challenges associated with this task?

2. Read and Review

- Carefully go through all the provided materials and instructions. Highlight key points and make notes on any unclear aspects that need further explanation.

3. Break Down the Task

- Divide the task into smaller, manageable steps. This will help you understand the sequence of actions required and ensure you don't overlook any critical components.

4. Set Personal Deadlines:

- Establish your own deadlines for each step of the task to keep yourself organized and on track.

5. Regular Feedback:

- Schedule periodic check-ins with your supervisor or client to provide updates and receive feedback. This keeps you aligned with their expectations and allows for adjustments as needed.

6. Seek Help When Needed:

- Don't hesitate to ask for help if you encounter obstacles or uncertainties. It's better to seek assistance early than to make avoidable mistakes.

7. Document Your Understanding:

- Write down your understanding of the task and review it with your supervisor or client. This ensures mutual agreement on the task's objectives and requirements.

Benefits of This Strategy:

- Increased Accuracy: Fully understanding the task reduces the likelihood of errors and ensures your work meets the required standards.
- Efficiency: A clear understanding leads to more efficient work processes, saving time and resources.
- Better Outcomes: When your efforts are aligned with the task's objectives and criteria for success, you are more likely to achieve positive results.
- Improved Communication Regularly seeking clarification and feedback enhances communication

with your supervisor or client, fostering better working relationships.

- Reduced Stress: Knowing exactly what needs to be done and why reduces anxiety and helps you work more confidently and comfortably

"Decipher to Deliver" is about taking the necessary steps to fully understand a task before diving into execution. By implementing this strategy, you can enhance your performance, ensure successful outcomes, and build a reputation for reliability and excellence in your professional environment.

Realm of Research

The research and studies across various fields consistently highlight the importance of clear task understanding for improving job performance, reducing errors, and enhancing job satisfaction. By adopting the "Decipher to Deliver" strategy, organizations and employees can achieve better outcomes, foster positive work environments, and drive overall success

There have been numerous studies and research papers that touch on the importance of understanding tasks before execution, particularly in the contexts of project management, employee performance, and organizational behavior. Here are a few key findings and studies that align with the principles of "Decipher to Deliver":

1. The Impact of Role Clarity on Job Satisfaction and Performance:

- A study published in the *Journal of Management* examined the relationship between role clarity and job satisfaction. The study found that employees who had a clear understanding of their roles and tasks were more satisfied with their jobs and performed better. This supports the idea that deciphering tasks before executing them can lead to better outcomes.

- Reference: Sawyer, J. E. (1992). "Goal and process clarity: Specification of multiple constructs of role ambiguity and a structural equation model of their antecedents and consequences." Journal of Applied Psychology, 77(2), 130-142.

2. The Role of Task Understanding in Reducing Errors:

- Research in cognitive psychology highlights that misunderstandings and lack of clarity about tasks are major contributors to errors and inefficiencies in work environments. Ensuring that employees fully understand their tasks before starting them can significantly reduce mistakes and improve overall efficiency.

- Reference: Reason, J. (2000). "Human error: Models and management." BMJ, 320(7237), 768-770.

3. Communication and Performance in Teams:

- A study in the *Academy of Management Journal* explored how effective communication within teams influences performance. The study concluded that clear communication of task expectations and objectives enhances team performance and cohesion. This finding underscores the importance of clarifying tasks before execution to ensure everyone is on the same page.

- Reference: Keller, R. T. (2001). Cross-functional project groups in research and new product development: Diversity, communications, job stress, and outcomes." Academy of Management Journal, 44(3), 547-555.

4. Project Management Best Practices:

- The Project Management Institute (PMI) has long advocated for the importance of defining project scope and objectives clearly at the outset. PMI's Project Management Body of Knowledge (PMBOK) emphasizes the need for clear task definitions and understanding to avoid scope creep and ensure project success.

- Reference: Project Management Institute. (2017). "A Guide to the Project Management Body of Knowledge (PMBOK Guide)." 6th Edition.

5. The Effect of Clarification on Employee Performance:

- An article in the *Harvard Business Review* discussed how leaders who take the time to clarify expectations and provide detailed task instructions can significantly enhance their team's performance. The article highlighted real-world examples of companies that saw improved performance metrics after implementing clearer communication strategies.

- Reference: Gallo, A. (2011). "The Value of Clear Communication in the Workplace." Harvard Business Review.

Job failure and project mishaps

While exact percentages can vary depending on the context and industry, it is evident from multiple studies that a significant proportion of job failures and project mishaps are related to poor understanding of tasks and expectations. These findings underscore the importance of strategies like "Decipher to Deliver" to enhance clarity, reduce errors, and improve overall performance.

several studies and surveys provide insights into how miscommunication and lack of role clarity contribute to job failure and project mishaps. Here are some key statistics:

1. Project Failure Due to Miscommunication

- According to a report by the Project Management Institute (PMI), poor communication is a primary factor in project failure, cited in 56% of the cases. Miscommunication often results from not understanding tasks clearly at the outset.

- Source: PMI, "The High Cost of Low Performance: The

Essential Role of Communications" (2013).

2. Employee Performance and Role Clarity

- A study conducted by Gallup found that only about 50% of employees strongly agree that they know what is expected of them at work. Lack of role clarity can lead to poor performance and job dissatisfaction.

- Source: Gallup, "State of the American Workplace" (2017).

3. Impact of Clarity on Performance:

- A survey by the Society for Human Resource Management (SHRM) revealed that 41% of employees felt their performance was negatively affected by unclear job expectations. This lack of clarity often stems from insufficient understanding of tasks.

- Source: SHRM, "2016 Employee Job Satisfaction and Engagement: Revitalizing a Changing Workforce."

4. Task Understanding in IT Projects:

- In the field of IT, a Standish Group report (Chaos Report) showed that only 29% of software development projects were completed successfully, with 19% failing outright. Many of these failures were attributed to incomplete understanding of project requirements and poor communication.

- Source: The Standish Group, "CHAOS Report" (2015).

5. Workplace Mistakes Due to Misunderstanding:

- A study published in the "Journal of Organizational Behavior" found that misunderstandings about tasks and expectations contributed to about 20-25% of workplace errors and inefficiencies.

- Source: Edmondson, A. C., & Nembhard, I. M. (2009). "Product development and learning in project teams: The challenges are the benefits." Journal of Organizational Behavior, 30(2), 201-225.

CHAPTER SEVENTEEN

Have a Promise to Yourself

The mantra of success begins with a simple yet profound commitment: have a promise to yourself. This foundational principle emphasizes the importance of self-reliance and personal integrity. By making a promise to yourself, you create a binding agreement that transcends external validations and expectations. It serves as a personal compass, guiding you through challenges and keeping you aligned with your goals and values.

This promise is not just about setting targets; it's about nurturing a steadfast commitment to your growth, well-being, and aspirations. It instills a sense of responsibility and accountability, driving you to persevere, overcome obstacles, and achieve excellence. In essence, having a promise to yourself is the cornerstone of building a life of purpose, resilience, and unwavering success.

The first step to make yourself best in the office is to promise yourself that you will be a changed you from this time onwards That's a great goal to have, and I'm happy to help you with some suggestions. As you all are aware , there are many ways you can make a difference at your work, depending on your goals and interests. Some of them are:

- Having a direct impact
- Supporting a positive-focused company
- Mentoring and transferring knowledge
- Fostering community
- Showing up positively
- Refusing to contribute to the negative
- Finding the meaning
- You can read more about these tips here, some more specific ideas, here are some examples of how you can apply these tips in your office:

1, If you want to have a direct impact,

you can look for opportunities to use your skills or talents to help others in your office or outside of it. For example, you could offer to help a coworker with a task they are struggling with, or you could join a volunteer project that your company supports.

2, If you want to support a positive-focused company,

you can research the mission, vision, and values of your company and see how they align with your own. You can also look for ways to contribute to the company's CSR program, such as participating in green initiatives, donating to charities, or raising awareness about social issues.

3, If you want to mentor and transfer knowledge,

you can share your knowledge and experience with others in your office, especially those who are new or less experienced than you. You can offer to mentor someone in your team or department or join a formal mentoring program in your company or industry. You can also create or contribute to knowledge bases, wikis, blogs, podcasts, or other platforms that can help others learn from you.

4, If you want to foster community,

you can build and maintain positive relationships with your coworkers, managers, clients, and stakeholders. You can show interest in their lives, listen to their concerns, offer support and feedback, and celebrate their achievements. You can also organize or participate in social events, team-building activities, networking sessions, or other opportunities to connect with others.

5, If you want to show up positively,

you can look for ways to be proactively positive in an authentic way. Admire someone's work on a project they just completed. Tell them. Know of a book you think someone would benefit from? Let them know about it. Even better, give them a copy. You can also express gratitude, appreciation, and recognition to those who deserve it.

6, If you want to refuse to contribute to the negative,

you can avoid or minimize negative behaviors that can harm the work environment or the morale of others. For example, you can refrain from gossiping, complaining, blaming, criticizing, or judging others. You can also challenge or report any unethical, unfair, or abusive conduct that you witness or experience.

7, If you want to find the meaning,

you can find meaning and purpose in your work, regardless of what you do. You can ask yourself how your work contributes to the bigger picture, what value it creates for others, and what skills or passions it allows you to use or develop.

8, You can also set personal or professional goals that motivate you and challenge you to grow.

These are just some examples of how you can make a difference in your office. Of course, there are many more ways that you can discover and explore on your own. The important thing is that you find what works for you and what makes you happy.

If you are a religious, God-fearing guy. you can create a promise or

a pledge of your own in the name of God, like this below...

Dear ....(your God's name),

I promise to work hard and be productive, not for the praise of men, but for the glory of your name. I will give my best effort to every task that I am assigned, and I will always strive to improve my skills and knowledge.

I will do this not to impress my boss or my colleagues, but to please you and to use my gifts to make a difference in the world. I promise to be reliable and trustworthy, because I know that you are watching over me. I will show up to work on time, meet my deadlines, and follow through on my commitments.

I will also be honest and ethical in all of my dealings with my colleagues and my boss. I know that you see everything that I do, and I want to live my life in a way that is pleasing to you. I promise to be positive and enthusiastic because I know that you have a good plan for my life. I will have a positive attitude towards my work, and I will be willing to help out my colleagues.

I will also be respectful and professional in my interactions with everyone in the workplace. I know that you have good things in store for me, and I want to be ready to receive them. I promise to be humble, because I know that I am nothing without you. I will not brag about my accomplishments, and I will not try to take credit for other people's work. I will also be willing to learn and grow from my mistakes.

I know that I am only where I am because of your grace, and I want to be grateful for everything that you have done for me. I promise to be forgiving

because I know that you have forgiven me. If I make a mistake, I will admit it and apologize. I will also be willing to forgive others for their mistakes. I know that you have forgiven me for all of my sins, and I want to be like you and

forgive others. I promise to be kind and compassionate because I know that you are kind and compassionate. I will be helpful and supportive of my colleagues,

and I will always treat everyone with respect. I know that you are kind and compassionate to me, and I want to be like you and show kindness and compassion to others.

I make this promise in your name, and I ask for your help in fulfilling it. I believe that if I follow these principles, I will be able to stand out in the office

and make a positive impact on my colleagues and my company. I also believe that I will be living a life that is pleasing to you and that is in line with your will for my life. Thank you for your guidance and your support.

I love you, God. ....

your name here

CHAPTER EIGHTEEN

Time is Trimmer

The Mantra "Time is Trimmer" encapsulates the idea of cutting away the unnecessary to streamline productivity and efficiency in an office setting. It suggests that managing time effectively is about trimming the excess, focusing on priorities, and eliminating waste. By adopting this mantra, one can achieve a leaner, more efficient workflow that maximizes output and minimizes distractions. It's a call to regularly review and refine work processes, prioritize tasks that add the most value, and continuously seek ways to optimize the use of time.

Effective time management is more than a matter of diligently checking off tasks on a to-do list. It's a holistic approach that empowers individuals to optimize their work hours, focus on high-priority tasks, and allocate resources efficiently. In an office setting, time management translates into heightened productivity, reduced stress, and a platform for professional growth.

In essence, effective time management encompasses a mindset shift from mere task completion to a strategic orchestration of one's workday. It involves understanding that time is a finite resource, and how it is utilized can significantly impact the quality of work, personal well-being, and career trajectory. This approach urges individuals to prioritize tasks based on their significance, allocate time in a way that maximizes output, and harness time as a valuable asset rather than a fleeting commodity.

Within the context of an office, this approach becomes even more critical. The intricate interplay of projects, deadlines, meetings, and collaborative efforts demands a methodical handling of time. Employees who master effective time management become adept at juggling these various demands, ensuring that each task is allocated the appropriate amount of time without sacrificing the quality of their work. This results in tasks being completed promptly, milestones achieved, and a consistent track record of reliability.

Furthermore, the positive impact of effective time management extends beyond the immediate realm of task completion. The reduction of last-minute rushes and unexpected workloads not only minimizes stress levels but also fosters mental clarity. Individuals who effectively manage their time are more likely to approach challenges with a calm and focused mindset, which in turn enhances problem-solving abilities and decision-making.

Avenue for Growth

Moreover, the practice of effective time management creates an avenue for personal growth and professional development. By allocating time for continuous learning, skill enhancement, and reflection, individuals can continually refine their expertise and stay attuned to industry trends. This dedication to improvement, facilitated by effective time management, can position individuals for career advancement and leadership roles within their organization. effective time management is a philosophy that transforms the way individuals approach their work, influencing their productivity, stress levels, and growth trajectory.

Tips and Strategies

In the modern office landscape, it serves as a linchpin for success, allowing individuals to navigate the complexities of their roles with poise, efficiency, and purpose. By embracing this mindset and employing the strategies that follow, employees and staff members can harness the power of time to elevate their professional journey. Effective time management is the practice of managing your work in order to ensure you're spending your time as intentionally as possible.

It can help you increase your productivity, reduce your stress, and achieve your goals. There are many tips and strategies for better time management, but here are some of the most common ones

SMART goals.

Setting SMART goals is a structured approach to goal-setting that helps you create clear, achievable, and well-defined objectives. SMART is an acronym that stands for Specific, Measurable, Achievable, Relevant, and Time-bound.

Here's how to set SMART goals:

1. Specific (S):

Your goal should be clear and specific, leaving no room for ambiguity. Clearly define what you want to accomplish and why it's important. Ask yourself the following questions:

- What exactly do I want to achieve?
- Why is this goal important?
- How will I achieve it?

1. Measurable (M):

Your goal should be quantifiable, allowing you to track your progress and determine when you've achieved it. Break your goal down into measurable components. Ask yourself:

- How will I measure my progress or know when the goal is achieved?
- What metrics or indicators can I use to track my success?
-

1. Achievable (A):

Your goal should be realistic and attainable given your resources, skills, and circumstances. While it's good to set challenging goals, ensure they are still feasible. Ask yourself:

- Is this goal realistic given my current resources and constraints?
- Do I have the necessary skills and support to achieve this goal?
-

3. Relevant (R):

your goal should align with your broader objectives and be relevant to your overall priorities. Consider whether the goal is meaningful and relevant to your personal or professional aspirations.

Ask yourself:

- Does this goal align with my values and long-term objectives?
- Will achieving this goal contribute to my overall mission or purpose?

4. Time-bound (T): Your goal should have a specific timeframe or deadline for completion. Setting a target date creates a sense of urgency and helps you stay focused. Ask yourself:

   - By when do I want to achieve this goal?
   - What is a realistic timeline for completing each step?

Putting it all together, let's say you have a goal to improve your fitness level: -

Specific: I want to improve my cardiovascular fitness and be able to run a 5K race. –

Measurable: I will track my progress by timing how long it takes me to run 1 mile and how many minutes I can sustain jogging without stopping. –

Achievable: I will start by jogging for 10 minutes and gradually increase my time each week. –

Relevant: Improving my fitness will enhance my overall health and well-being. –

Time-bound: I will be ready to run a 5K race in three months. I

will increase my jogging time by 2 minutes each week.

By setting SMART goals, you create a roadmap for success that is well-defined, manageable, and aligned with your aspirations. Regularly reviewing and adjusting your SMART goals can help you stay on track and achieve meaningful outcomes.

Prioritize your tasks.

Prioritizing tasks is essential for effective time management and productivity. Here's a step-by-step guide on how to prioritize your tasks:

Make a List: Start by listing all the tasks you need to complete. Include

both work-related and personal tasks.

Identify Deadlines: Highlight tasks with specific deadlines. These

tasks should take precedence as they have a set time frame for completion.

Evaluate Importance: Assess the importance of each task. Consider

factors such as the impact the task has on your goals, projects,

or responsibilities.

Consider Urgency: Determine the urgency of each task. Some tasks might

be important but not urgent, while others might require immediate attention.

Use the Eisenhower Matrix: This

matrix categorizes tasks into four quadrants based on importance and

urgency: Urgent and Important: Do these tasks first.

1. Important but Not Urgent: Schedule these tasks for later.
2. Urgent but Not Important: Delegate these tasks if possible.
3. Not Urgent and Not Important: Consider eliminating or
4. postponing these tasks.
5. Estimate Effort: Estimate the time and effort required for each task.

This will help you allocate appropriate time slots for them.

Consider Dependencies: Some tasks might be dependent on others

being completed first. Identify these dependencies and prioritize

accordingly.

Use the ABCD Method:

Assign priorities using the ABCD method:

A: High priority, must be done today.

B: Should be done today but not as critical as A tasks.

C: Can be done today, but not essential.

D: Delegate tasks that can be done by someone else.

Apply the 80/20 Rule: The Pareto Principle states that 80% of results come from 20% of efforts. Focus on tasks that contribute most to your goals and outcomes.

Consider Energy Levels: Schedule tasks based on your energy levels throughout the day. Do high-energy tasks when you're most alert and lower-energy tasks during less productive times.

Break Down Large Tasks: If a task seems overwhelming, break it into smaller, manageable sub-tasks. This makes it easier to prioritize and tackle.

Create a Schedule: Based on your assessments, create a daily or weekly schedule that outlines when you'll work on each task.

Reevaluate and Adjust: Regularly review and adjust your task priorities as new information comes in or circumstances change.

Be Realistic: Avoid overloading yourself with too many high-priority tasks in a short timeframe. Be realistic about what you can accomplish. **Learn to Say No**: If new tasks come up that don't align with your current priorities, consider whether you can take them on without sacrificing existing commitments.

Use Productivity Tools: Consider using digital tools or apps to help you manage and prioritize tasks, set reminders, and track progress. **Celebrate Progress:** Acknowledge and celebrate your accomplishments, even if they're small. This can boost motivation and maintain a positive outlook. prioritization is an ongoing process. As your complete tasks and new ones arise, continually assess and adjust your priorities to ensure you're focusing your time and energy on what matters most.

Plan your time.

Once you have your goals and priorities clear, you can create a schedule or a calendar that outlines how you will spend your time on different tasks and activities. You can use tools like Asana or Google Calendar to plan your time and set reminders for deadlines and events. You can also use time blocking or batching techniques to group similar tasks together and allocate specific time slots for them. While achieving perfect time management may be challenging, you can certainly improve your time management skills and create a more effective and efficient schedule. Here's a guide to help you plan your time effectively:

1. Set Clear Goals: Define your short-term and long-term goals. Knowing what you want to achieve will guide your time management efforts and help you prioritize tasks.

2. Create a To-Do List: Make a list of tasks you need to complete. Include both work-related and personal tasks. Break down larger tasks into smaller, actionable steps.

3. Use a Planner or Digital Tool: Choose a planner, calendar, or digital task management tool to organize your

tasks and schedule. Use whatever

method works best for you.

4. Apply the methods mentioned earlier, such as the Eisenhower Matrix or the ABCD method, to prioritize tasks based on their importance and

urgency.

5. Allocate Time Blocks: Assign specific time blocks for different tasks. Be realistic about how much time each task will take. Consider your energy

levels and concentration span throughout the day.

6. Time Blocking: Allocate specific time blocks for different types of tasks. For example, designate a block for focused work, another for meetings, and another for breaks.

7. Batch Similar Tasks: Group similar tasks together and complete them during a designated time block. This minimizes context switching and improves efficiency.

8. Eliminate Distractions: During your focused work time, eliminate distractions. Put away your phone, close unrelated tabs on your computer, and create a quiet workspace.

9. Use the Pomodoro Technique: Work in focused intervals, typically 25 minutes, followed by a short break. This technique can help maintain concentration and prevent burnout.

10. Be Realistic: Avoid overloading your schedule. Leave some buffer time

for unexpected tasks or interruptions.

11.Learn to Say No: Don't overcommit yourself. Politely decline tasks or projects that don't align with your current priorities.

12. Review and Reflect: At the end of each day or week, review your progress. Celebrate accomplishments and

identify areas for improvement.

13. Weekly Planning: Dedicate time at the beginning of each week to plan the upcoming week's tasks and schedule.

14. Monthly and Quarterly Goals: Set bigger goals for the month or quarter and break them down into actionable steps. This helps you stay on track with your long-term objectives.

15. Delegate: If possible, delegate tasks that others can handle. This frees up your time for higher-priority tasks.

16. Self-Care: Schedule time for self-care activities, exercise, relaxation, and spending time with loved ones. Taking care of your well-being enhances your overall productivity.

17. Flexibility: Be prepared to adjust your plan as needed. Unexpected events can arise, so having a flexible mindset is essential.

18. Continuous Learning: Keep improving your time management skills. Explore new techniques and strategies that align with your needs and preferences.

19. Celebrate Achievements: Acknowledge your achievements and milestones. Celebrating your progress boosts motivation and positivity.

Remember, the goal is effective time management, not necessarily perfection.

Adapt these strategies to your unique circumstances and consistently practice them to improve your time management skills over time.

www.ingramcontent.com/pod-product-compliance
Lightning Source LLC
LaVergne TN
LVHW021155160826
845679LV00024B/2137

* 9 7 9 8 8 9 4 4 6 7 1 5 3 *